Drew pulled her close against him, kissing her lightly. "And I want to be the one who teaches you how magical it can be."

"We don't even know each other." Laurel felt herself being pulled deeper and deeper. "Nobody falls in love that fast."

"I know all the important things about you," he retorted significantly. "I know you don't snore and you squeeze the toothpaste from the bottom, exactly like I do."

"You really are obstinate!"

"I also know that you have a very nasty temper."

"No worse than yours!" she flared.

"See what I mean?" He grinned broadly.

Drew stroked the length of her slim legs, his hands soothing the taut muscles, his lips teasing gently at the corner of her mouth. Laurel turned her mouth to his kiss, putting her arms around his neck, not making any attempt to escape...

Dear Reader:

As the months go by, we continue to receive word from you that SECOND CHANCE AT LOVE romances are providing you with the kind of romantic entertainment you're looking for. In your letters you've voiced enthusiastic support for SECOND CHANCE AT LOVE, you've shared your thoughts on how personally meaningful the books are, and you've suggested ideas and changes for future books. Although we can't always reply to your letters as quickly as we'd like, please be assured that we appreciate your comments. Your thoughts are all-important to us!

We're glad many of you have come to associate SECOND CHANCE AT LOVE books with our butterfly trademark. We think the butterfly is a perfect symbol of the reaffirmation of life and thrilling new love that SECOND CHANCE AT LOVE heroines and heroes find together in each story. We hope you keep asking for the "butterfly books," and that, when you buy one—whether by a favorite author or a talented new writer—you're sure of a good read. You can trust all SECOND CHANCE AT LOVE books to live up to the high standards of romantic fiction you've come to expect.

So happy reading, and keep your letters coming!

With warm wishes,

Ellen Edwards

Ellen Edwards
SECOND CHANCE AT LOVE
The Berkley/Jove Publishing Group
200 Madison Avenue
New York, NY 10016

Second Chance at Love®

IN THE ARMS
OF A STRANGER
DEBORAH JOYCE

A
SECOND CHANCE AT LOVE
BOOK

IN THE ARMS OF A STRANGER

First edition published March 1983

First printing

"Second Chance at Love" and the butterfly emblem are trademarks be-
longing to Jove Publications, Inc.

Printed in the United States of America

Second Chance at Love books are published by
The Berkley/Jove Publishing Group
200 Madison Avenue, New York, NY 10016

For Gary and Ken,
who never stopped believing

CHAPTER ONE

TRAFFIC WAS UNUSUALLY heavy for this time of day, the hot, muggy air mingling with exhaust from idling cars whose drivers waited impatiently for the light to turn green. Laurel Grey drummed her fingers nervously on the steering wheel of her small car, glancing at her watch and wincing as she noted the time.

Almost nine, and she'd promised to meet Howard for dinner at seven-thirty. She hoped he'd gotten the message she'd telephoned. A heated debate on current economic headaches had kept her longer than she'd expected at the conference of small newspaper owners being held this week in Wilmington.

As the signal changed and the hovering cars surged forward, Laurel sighed restlessly. Her chances of getting any dinner this late were extremely remote; Howard was certain to have eaten already.

Howard Ashley was her distant cousin; "kissing cousins" they called them here in North Carolina. Whenever she was in town they dined together, usually at one of the excellent seafood restaurants for which the area was noted. Howard had suggested they meet tonight at a private club he'd recently joined. The food was delicious, he'd told her, his voice sounding unusually enthusiastic for him.

Laurel maneuvered quickly through the traffic, ignoring several blaring horns as she cut across two lanes to make a right turn. Yes, there it was: a large gray building built of weathered boards, sheltered beneath a cluster of discreetly lit white oak trees. It was surrounded by cars, and she had to circle the lot several times before finding a parking space.

A quick inspection of her face in the rearview mirror did nothing to sweeten her mood. She hadn't even stopped to comb her thick, chestnut brown hair when she left the meeting, wanting only to get to the club as fast as possible. Beneath straight, dark brows her own blue eyes stared back at her, their color deepened to a rich azure in the dim light. She wasn't beautiful, at least not by cover-girl standards, but her high cheekbones and finely shaped mouth had their own attraction, she assured herself.

The fabric of her camel linen pantsuit clung limply to her slim figure as she walked rapidly to the door, and Laurel hoped the interior would be shadowy. Luckily Howard wasn't fussy about how she dressed. He was an even-tempered man, calm and placid, but he wouldn't be happy about being kept waiting this long.

She grasped the handle of the oversized, heavy wooden door, hesitating briefly as a firm, masculine arm reached past her and swung it open. Looking back in surprise, she encountered an intent pair of coppery brown eyes that were inspecting her slender length with a stripping glance.

He was a tall, lean man, youngish but definitely over thirty. A navy blue cotton shirt, open at the collar, emphasized his darkly tanned skin and thick brown hair. Laurel did not care for the faint insolent smile he was giving her.

"After you," he murmured, the smile lighting the depths of his eyes. He moved closer and placed one hand lightly against her back.

It was the last straw in a hectic, infuriating day, one in which she'd repeatedly been forced to defend her status in a series of male-dominated meetings. Although the owner and editor of one of coastal North Carolina's oldest weekly newspapers, Laurel still had to fight a constant battle to be taken seriously by her male counterparts. She was in no mood to deal with another arrogant man at this moment, particularly one on the prowl.

"I don't need any assistance in getting through the door," she snapped, deliberately moving away from his light touch.

The words barely left her lips before the door swung shut behind her, slamming against her back and propelling her into the building with startling force. She braced one hand against the nearest wall, trying to keep her balance, but the floor seemed to leap up and make resounding contact with her rump. The door swung open again. As Laurel looked up in stunned surprise, the man stepped past her, laughing quietly as he flung over his shoulder, "Need any assistance now?"

"You creep," she hissed angrily, getting to her feet and quickly moving past him. Her heels clicked furiously against the polished wooden floor as she crossed the wide entry hall and stopped at the door of the dining room.

"May I help you?" There was a polite chill in the way the words were spoken, and Laurel turned to find the maître d' hovering behind her, his gaze summing up her appearance in her simple business suit and dismissing her importance before she could even reply.

"Mr. Howard Ashley is expecting me," she bit out.

"I'll check," he replied, disappearing into the dimly lit room in front of them. Laurel waited impatiently for him to return, still smarting from her encounter at the door. Perhaps she had been unnecessarily brusque with that man, but the day had drained her tolerance to a low ebb. And the fact that many hours had elapsed since her last meal didn't improve her disposition at all.

The maître d' returned. "Mr. Ashley doesn't appear to be in the dining room. Have you tried the game-room?" A nod of his head indicated the way, and he turned and walked away without waiting for her reply.

It seemed unlikely to her that Howard would be found in the game-room. The only games she ever remembered seeing him play were ones designed to entertain the small patients he catered to in his newly established practice as a children's dentist. She moved down the hallway, glancing around the designated area.

At the end of the corridor she paused before taking a turn that led her to the doorway of a dark room. It was hazy blue with the smoke of innumerable cigarettes, the air filled with that peculiar combination of murmured conversation and clinking ice cubes that characterizes an expensive private club.

This wasn't her scene at all, and it certainly wasn't where she would expect to find Howard. Most of the women were dressed in silky trousers and sequined camisole tops that sparkled under the track-lights beaming onto the long velvet-covered table in the center of the room. There seemed to be more men than women, their body-hugging trousers and casually elegant shirts blending smoothly into the dim shadows.

Two men came in behind her, laughing and talking loudly as they passed, pausing to give her quick assessing glances that were in keeping with the mood of the club. This was one of Wilmington's newest attractions, an intimate little club where singles came to chase away loneliness and find informal entertainment. Board games were being played on the midnight black table, but that wasn't where the real scoring took place, Laurel surmised.

Laurel's irritation level rose another notch as she stared coolly back at the men until they moved on. Where on earth was Howard? With the light shining behind her, she was afraid it looked as if she were deliberately seeking attention.

Slowly she circled the table, finding it difficult to glimpse the faces of the couples bent over the game boards. Many of them were playing backgammon, and here and there waitresses leaned over to set down fresh drinks on the black velvet. There was no obvious exchange of money. Drinks went onto the member's tab, and the help stayed in the background. Apparently nothing was allowed to distract one from the main purpose of the club.

Unexpectedly she caught sight of Howard's sandy hair. She started toward him and then stopped. Beside him sat a blonde, her hair twisted into a gleaming coil above wide blue eyes and baby smooth skin. Their faces were close together, their hands almost touching. As a burst of laughter erupted nearby, Laurel slid into the closest empty chair. She had no intention of interrupting such an intimate encounter.

"Tired of going it alone?" The words were murmured silkily beside her, and Laurel turned sharply. Brown eyes teased her, laughing as her initial surprise changed to annoyance. Damn, how could she have been such a fool as to not look where she was sitting? It would be her luck to pick the seat next to the man she'd so rudely encountered in the doorway.

"I'm waiting for my date," she said icily, emphasizing the last word with deliberation.

"Isn't everyone?" he ventured affably. "What game would you like to play?" Taking his time, he allowed his eyes to roam over her, finally stopping to gaze into the eyes that glared back at him with fury.

"Not the one you have in mind," Laurel countered angrily, forcing herself not to flinch as she coolly returned the appraising gaze. Her first impression of the man had been right. A flirt, obviously looking for someone to share the evening. Well, even without Howard to consider, she wasn't interested in this man's brazen charm.

If she'd hoped to anger him with her remark, she failed. He grinned at her, saying, "Has anyone ever told you your voice is very sexy?"

"Do you have much success with that line?" she retorted.

"You'd be surprised." His nonchalant smile didn't alter, his eyes again running over her in lazy assessment. He followed up by reaching for one of the game boards and sliding it in front of them. "We're a little conspicuous without a game. How about letting me teach you Pente? Like love, it's easy to learn but hard to master."

"A personal observation of yours?" Laurel glared back at him, unwilling to admit she'd never heard of the game.

"Sorry, it's the motto of the game." Picking up a velvet pouch, he spilled out jewel-colored translucent glass stones, his slender but powerful-looking fingers dividing them and sliding half in front of her.

She was tempted to get up and walk away, but there were no other empty chairs on this side of the room. After a quick glance to confirm that Howard was still busily engaged over his own game, she said, "If you're trying to be helpful, perhaps you could attract the attention of a waitress."

The man beside her gracefully rose and lifted a hand. His efforts were instantly rewarded as one of the scantily clad waitresses made her way toward them. Laurel spoke in clipped tones: "Any possibility of getting something to eat?"

"I can bring over a snack tray," the girl replied. "What would you like to drink?"

"A wine cooler," Laurel replied, uncomfortably aware of her companion's intense scrutiny. Seeing that he already had a drink, the waitress moved off.

He spoke again. "Do you have a name?"

"Yes," she flashed.

"Strange, I would have sworn it was no," he drawled. "Mine's Drew."

Laurel smiled unwillingly, relenting somewhat, aware that her churlish manner was related as much to hunger as to anything else. "I'm Laurel." She fingered one of the stones in front of her, sliding it around aimlessly. If Howard hadn't noticed her by the time she finished eating she'd write a note and have the waitress deliver it. Considering how dependable he was, there was no way he would leave until he heard from her.

She and Howard made a good couple, she reflected. He saw past her own threatening facade, laughing gently at the way men seemed to draw back under her cool, direct gaze. A lifelong friendship between them had slowly drifted into a dating arrangement, which would probably culminate in marriage someday, although the thought was still unspoken. The fact that he was enjoying the company of another woman right now didn't bother her. They had a relationship free of strings, free of possessiveness. Perhaps that was because their emotions weren't deeply involved, she suddenly realized.

The waitress returned with a tray of small sandwiches and, looking toward Drew, asked, "What is the name, please?"

Before he could speak Laurel interrupted hastily. "Ashley," she said firmly, and the waitress moved off again. Laurel attacked several of the delicate morsels without delay, refusing to meet the sardonic glance of the man beside her. When the edge was taken off her hunger she took several sips of her wine, continuing to glance in Howard's direction at regular intervals.

"If you ask me, he's taken," Drew finally observed, his brown eyes teasing. "Do you know him, or are you just looking?"

Laurel looked at him with amusement. The whole world looked better now that she'd eaten. "He's my date," she explained. "I can't expect him to wait nearly two hours without getting a little bored, but sometimes work won't wait."

"You, too?" Drew nodded his head in Howard's direction. "Your friend is with my date. He must be entertaining, or April would probably be in a temper."

Laurel inspected the blonde more closely. A cloud of pale hair surrounded a dramatically made-up face, which was dominated by a sensual mouth. Mounds of creamy flesh spilled over the top of a black strapless satin jumpsuit that molded itself to her voluptuous curves. She was the type of woman Laurel could have guessed this man would choose: someone whose blatant sexuality would complement his rugged masculinity.

"Ready for that game?" he prompted, watching her as she pushed away her glass.

"Only if it's as easy to learn as you promised. This has been a long day."

"Nothing to it," he assured. "We each get forty playing stones." Pointing to a board covered with grid lines, he continued, "The game is a natural for one of these clubs. Its principles are chase and retreat, attack and retreat, capture and build. Then it's 'I've got you.'"

Laurel laughed, enjoying his play on words and reluctantly acknowledging that he could probably be an interesting companion. She saw a decided interest leap in the dark eyes studying her, and she instantly regretted her friendliness. He was probably piqued over being ignored by the blonde and was looking for someone to build up his wounded ego. "Don't count on it," she added firmly.

They had been playing only a few minutes when Howard looked up and saw her. He pushed back his chair hastily. At the same moment the blonde caught sight of Laurel's companion and rushed over, draping her luscious body against him and lowering her face for his kiss.

Laurel tensed and turned toward Howard, barely hearing his profuse apologies for not having seen her arrival.

By the time he finished speaking the other couple had disappeared and Laurel felt a momentary flicker of regret. It would be useless to try to tell herself she hadn't enjoyed the encounter. Perhaps it was only because Drew had been a challenge.

She turned toward Howard, forcing herself to forget the other man. "I'm the one who should be offering excuses. I thought I'd never break loose from that last meeting."

"Then you must be starving," he sympathized. "Tell me all about it over dinner."

Howard had not eaten, explaining he preferred waiting for her to join him. They went back to the quiet dining room, starting their meal with bowls of steaming clam chowder and a delicate white wine recommended by the waiter.

The room was elegantly furnished, the service excellent, and the food as delicious as Howard had promised. "Your dental practice must be flourishing," Laurel murmured, indicating the opulence of their surroundings.

Howard flushed with pleasure at her praise. "It's important to look successful," he explained.

"Was that the purpose of the blonde?" Laurel couldn't resist the temptation to tease.

His pink skin deepened to scarlet. "She came over and sat down beside me," he protested.

"And I can't blame her," Laurel said soothingly, surprised that Howard was upset. He must have liked the blonde. For a moment Laurel was tempted to ask if he was acquainted with Drew. It would be interesting to see how the facts tallied with her initial assessment, but the thought of Howard's curiosity stopped her. She was in no mood to have her own reactions to the man examined.

"Did you hear anything useful at the conference?" he quizzed.

"I learned that most weekly papers like mine are struggling to exist. In fact, *The Beacon* sounded almost prosperous compared to others I heard about."

With a burst of emotion unusual for Howard he exclaimed, "Then why do you kill yourself putting it out?"

Laurel carefully buttered a thick slice of rye bread before answering. "Because I love it. The newspaper business is in my blood. You can't imagine the excitement I feel when the advertising's satisfactory, the columns are checked, my editorial's finished, and press deadline nears! It's worth all the late nights and missed dates and the lack of money..." Her voice trailed off as she eyed Howard defensively.

He shrugged with a gesture of defeat. "I'm sorry, Laurel. If it makes you happy, then it seems harmless enough to me."

Harmless? Laurel felt her blood pressure rise perceptibly at the patronizing remark. How would he feel if she brushed off his work so casually? She reached for her glass of wine and took several cooling sips. Arguing with Howard was stupid. He always ended up apologizing and making her feel ashamed of her own steamroller tactics.

"It's probably because of your close relationship with your father," he was continuing, offering the remark as an excuse for her emotional outburst.

Laurel nodded in resignation. She and her father had been closer than most. From the time she learned to walk she had followed her father around their small North

Carolina town, learning to recognize newsworthy stories. She'd followed in his footsteps all the way to being editor of the town's only paper.

The busboy arrived to remove their empty soup bowls, and the waiter followed to replace them with plates of spicy curried chicken over wild rice.

"Any chance you'll be free next weekend? We could go to the sailing regatta at Beaufort." Howard's good humor was in evidence again as he extended the invitation.

Laurel's eyes expressed regret as they met his. "Sorry, but I'm going to the lighthouse," she said.

"Why?" he asked in obvious surprise.

"I haven't been there in a while, and I need a weekend to relax and get some rest." Laurel pushed her food around her plate, no longer hungry. The lighthouse was one of her major headaches right now. An old structure, it had stood on the North Carolina coast for almost one hundred years since Laurel's own great-uncle had built it. Her father had turned that section of beach over to the town before he died, and since then it had become a popular picnic site. In the past few months there had been several attempts by a large development corporation to acquire the land as a building site for condominiums, a plan Laurel violently opposed.

"Are you the only one who still visits the old place?" Howard was surveying his meal rather than looking at her.

"Not at all. It's a regular field trip for the local schools, and picknickers love that section of beach." Laurel warmed to her favorite subject.

"Then why are you so worried about those rumors it might be sold?"

"I'm afraid it might be more than a rumor this time. There've been rumblings about a concrete offer being made."

"I suppose you're going to fight it," Howard countered, resignation lacing his voice.

Laurel leaned forward, her voice catching fire. "I'm going to fight it with every ounce of strength I have."

"Good for you," Howard responded evenly. Laurel sensed that he had lost interest, so she changed the subject. For the rest of the meal they discussed mutual friends and an upcoming ballet production at the restored Thalian Hall, Wilmington's prize landmark.

When Laurel suggested they leave, explaining she needed to return to her hotel and work on some notes for the next day's conference, Howard looked almost relieved. Probably facing a busy schedule himself, Laurel surmised as he walked her to her car and kissed her lightly. She drove away without a backward glance.

It had been an extravagance to book a room at the hotel when her own home was only an hour's drive away, but she knew there was no hope of concentrating on the conference if she went home each evening and confronted the daily problems of the newspaper. Now she was glad she wasn't facing a long drive at such a late hour.

The hotel lobby was nearly deserted when she entered and crossed to the elevator. While she waited for it to descend from an upper floor the desk clerk came over and handed her a message. "Joe Barnes called," the note read.

Damn. A call from Joe tonight could mean only trouble. He was her one full-time employee, and although his main job was that of pressman, he filled in on a number of other tasks.

When she reached her room, she dialed the number, drumming her fingers anxiously as she listened to it ring. When Joe finally answered he launched right into business. "Sorry to bother you, Laurel, but Mrs. Macon has been phoning all evening. She says you promised to put her notice of the garden club's rummage sale on the front page and—"

"I told her plainly it would have to go under the Notices column unless she paid the advertising rates," Laurel protested tiredly.

"I know," Joe laughed. "I thought maybe you'd want to call and soothe her ruffled feathers. Your father always thought it helped to show a little personal sympathy, even if you couldn't do what they asked."

Laurel sighed. "You're right, Joe. Give me her number and I'll ring her first thing in the morning." Joe was a short, stocky, red-faced man of indeterminate age who had run the presses for as long as Laurel could remember. He and Laurel's father had been the best of friends, and Laurel always acknowledged the wisdom of his advice.

Hanging up the phone, she slowly stripped off her rumpled clothes and dragged herself into the bathroom. After turning on the faucets over the gleaming tub, she brushed her thick chestnut hair until it tumbled around her shoulders. There was a strange restlessness inside her, unrelated to her usual concerns over work or the overwhelming mass of information she'd absorbed during today's conference sessions.

Her thoughts kept straying to her encounter with Drew. Why had he had such an impact on her? Was it sheer sexual magnetism, body chemistry? He was an attractive man; but she met plenty of attractive men in her daily course of work and none of them made any lasting impression on her. From the little she'd seen of Drew she guessed he was a dominating, forceful man who exercised his allure with deliberate control.

Sliding into the tub, she relaxed in the warm water, stretching out her slim legs and trying to ease the tension in her tired muscles. For some reason, meeting Drew had made her remember Vince, something she tried not to do. Was there a resemblance between the two men? Not physically, of course, but there seemed to be a determined, hard edge underlying Drew's manner that made her recall that painful episode in her past.

She'd fallen for Vince almost on their first date. He was rugged and handsome, a man who exuded charm. Only later had she learned his charm was an excuse for a profound lack of ability. He'd also been ruthless and cruel, but she hadn't suspected that at first either. Thrilled over his attentions, she'd let him fill a void in her life created by the death of her father only months before her nineteenth birthday.

As a freelance writer Vince had been more than willing to accept her offer of a job to help out on the paper during those difficult weeks of struggle after her father's sudden death. At first it had seemed they made a perfect couple, sharing an interest in newspaper work, busily planning their future in journalism. When he'd asked her to marry him, she'd accepted eagerly, quelling the niggling doubts that cropped up in the back of her mind.

Perhaps if she had been older, or not so lonely after the loss of her father, she would have seen her attraction to Vince for what it was. Her need for closeness, for love, had blinded her, making her powerless in the face of Vince's domination. In the painful months following their wedding, Vince had quickly become dissatisfied with the restrictions of life in Laurel's hometown, blaming her for his own restlessness, finding an outlet for his frustrations by proving his influence over her life.

Almost imperceptibly he'd begun taking control, sending out tentacles of possessiveness that wrapped themselves around every facet of Laurel's life, cunningly stifling her wishes, smothering her thoughts, snuffing out her identity until only a shadow remained.

And Laurel had finally realized that Vince had no conscience; he pursued other women relentlessly. He had no respect for them, seeing women only as objects to be used and then discarded. His casual mention of conquests when he returned from frequent out-of-town trips sickened her, making it impossible for her to respond to his selfish, unfeeling lovemaking.

The phone call telling her of the light plane crash that had claimed Vince's life and that of the woman with him had left her confused and humiliated. In the following weeks Laurel had longed for some measure of privacy, a retreat from the sympathy and curiosity of her neighbors.

She'd buried herself in work, determined never to share her life so fully with another man, painstakingly reclaiming her own identity and even going so far as to take back her family name. As time passed she managed to shut out that year of her life, remembering as little as possible. The newspaper had barely survived, its resources drained by Vince's reckless spending and lack of interest. Laurel had devoted all her time to fighting for its existence, pushing aside all other elements of her life.

Only someone like Howard had a place in her life now—a man who offered no surprises, no strange twists, no unknown factors that could overturn her life, destroy the things important to her, leave her vulnerable and open to domination. Family, love, and companionship were all priorities, but not with someone who claimed superiority and equated sexual prowess with masculinity.

That must be why she felt so disturbed tonight. Drew had rattled the protective shield she'd built around herself, forced her to an awareness of feelings she didn't want to remember, reopened old wounds. It wasn't difficult to picture the type of man he would be. If a woman appealed to him, he'd probably get her into bed with precious few preliminaries. How was it he'd described it? Chase, attack, then "I've got you."

No, thank you. She wasn't available. Independence meant too much to permit herself to become a pawn in any man's mating game.

CHAPTER TWO

RAIN WAS ALREADY beginning to fall from gray, cloud-covered skies as Laurel sat restlessly behind her desk, thumping a pencil idly against the space bar of her ancient typewriter. Her hair, caught low at the back of her neck in a tortoise-shell barrette, swung foward as she leaned to look once again at her pile of scribbled notes. The storm outside was making it impossible for her to concentrate on the notations she'd made at a meeting of the town council earlier in the day.

A sudden streak of lightning lit up the corners of the dusty room followed a moment later by a thunder clap that rattled the thick plate-glass windows that made up one wall of the office. Excited by the storm, Laurel jumped up and hurried over to the door, pressing her nose against the glass and trying to see out between the stenciled black letters proclaiming this the office of her newspaper, *The Beacon*.

Rain was coming down in sheets now, pelting the sidewalk and running in rivulets down the wide main street of town. A woman was hurrying across the street, attempting to shield herself against the punishing downpour with a flimsy plastic umbrella. Laurel stepped back quickly and grasped the door, opening it a little way and peering out. The other woman swept into the room and stood gasping for a moment, water dripping from her curly brown hair.

"What are you doing out in this rain?" Laurel chided, surveying her best friend's bedraggled state.

"I have the most awful news!" Joan Farrel slipped out of her raincoat and laid it carefully over the front counter before continuing. "The telephone lines are down, but I just had to catch you. Surely you're not going to the lighthouse *this* weekend!"

Joan's abrupt change of subject didn't surprise Laurel; her friend always kept her biggest news for last. "Rain or not, nothing is going to spoil this weekend for me," Laurel affirmed. As Joan ran a comb through her wet hair Laurel frowned thoughtfully. "I've been planning on getting away all week. Last weekend was entirely taken up by the conference, and the thought of two whole lovely days to do as I please was the only thing that got me through hours of meetings—and helped me deal with that antiquated press, which naturally decided to break down three times since I returned. I'm going to reward myself with a weekend at the beach even if I have to swim all the way there!"

Tucking some straying hair back into her barrette, she hooked one thumb over the belt of her faded jeans and waited for Joan's arguments. She and Joan had been friends for years, drawn together by the fact that both of them had lost their mothers early in life. Laurel, the older at twenty-eight, was used to the way Joan dramatized things. When Joan simply shrugged her shoulders expressively, Laurel sighed before continuing patiently, "Why don't we go upstairs? You can tell me your news while I make some coffee."

They went up the narrow steps at the back of the shop and entered a second-floor apartment, where the Grey family had lived ever since Laurel's great-grandfather founded the small country newspaper. Joan flopped down into a large upholstered chair and leaned back. "Thank goodness it's Friday. At least we don't have to get to work in this rain tomorrow."

Laurel was busy in the tiny kitchen, setting a kettle on the gas stove and spooning instant coffee into two mugs. "Is it supposed to rain all weekend?" she called before returning to lean against the doorjamb.

"At least until tomorrow night." Joan's voice was cross and tired.

"You look exhausted." Laurel eyed her friend with concern. Joan's usually calm face was paler than usual. "Are things all right between you and Pete?"

Joan's eyes gleamed with enthusiasm at the mention of her longtime boyfriend. "Everything's fine. We're going out tonight. I'm just tired because the mayor has worked me hard all week. You know how he is when election time rolls around. As if anyone else would want his job!"

"Have you and Pete set a wedding date yet?" Laurel's tone was mildly teasing. Usually Joan talked nonstop about Pete, never seeming to mind that family problems had prevented them from marrying so far.

"We're hoping for a spring wedding." Joan's face shone with happiness. Suddenly the vision of her feminine loveliness in her frilly blouse and soft skirt made

Laurel uncomfortably aware of her own drab shirt and jeans.

"Fantastic!" Laurel said warmly. "As soon as you know the date, let me know and I'll print it on the front page."

Joan laughed appreciatively before saying, "So you're still planning to stay out at the lighthouse in this weather, are you?"

Laurel turned to shut off the gas burner and pour steaming water into the mugs before carrying the tray across to a heavy oak table beside the couch. "You know how I love storms," she said, ignoring her friend's worried frown. Deciding she'd humored Joan in her procrastination long enough, she handed her one of the mugs and settled back on the couch. "Now, what's your awful news?"

Joan took several irritatingly long swallows of her coffee before answering. "As a matter of fact, it's something to do with the lighthouse. J. A. Lockner submitted his final bid for the property to the town council this afternoon, and the price he's offering is too good for them to refuse. It looks like he's going to get the land."

"They can't sell!" Laurel's voice rippled with shock and anger. "I thought they agreed this morning they wouldn't sell to the Lockner Development Corporation under any circumstances." Her hands were shaking a little, and she winced as coffee sloshed over the rim of her mug, burning through the worn fabric of her jeans.

"This morning they didn't know how much money he was offering," Joan said dryly.

"But they know what he plans to do with the land. He's going to build one of those damn condominiums of his and ruin our beach." Laurel felt a rampant hostility begin to build inside her. This very morning the mayor had invited her to the town council meeting, assuring her they were not going to sell the land.

"His buildings are really quite attractive." Joan's voice was slightly pleading. As secretary to Mayor Boggs, she was caught between her loyalty to her boss and her friendship with Laurel.

"They're horrible," Laurel pronounced firmly. "He's already covered the beach with them from here to Wilmington, and now he wants to spoil our town as well."

"Lockner's promised he won't tear down the lighthouse." Joan was plainly trying to avoid an argument.

"Maybe he won't tear it down, but who'll be able to see it once he builds a huge concrete-and-glass structure right beside it?" Laurel forced her voice to remain calm, but inside she was furious. She could even feel a tiny pulse beating against her forehead.

"He's got an awfully sexy voice," Joan said lightly. "At least he sounded quite interesting on the telephone."

Laurel didn't bother to respond to that remark, and they sipped their coffee in silence for a few minutes. "You'd think an architect with a background like his would design nicer apartment buildings," Laurel said finally. "Hasn't he won several awards for his office parks?"

"Mayor Boggs told me Mr. Lockner is quite an artist," Joan agreed. "In fact, he planned to study art in college before his father died."

Laurel was curious in spite of herself. "Why did that stop him?"

"He was left with massive debts, which could be paid off only by fulfilling the company's contracts."

"His father founded the company?" Laurel asked.

"Only about two years before he died," Joan explained. "You have to admire Lockner for paying off those debts. He left Duke University and went home to Wilmington. It was five years before he had a chance to go back to college, and then he studied architecture."

"You do the admiring while I save my lighthouse," Laurel said dryly.

After an awkward pause Joan changed the subject. "You're getting too thin, Laurel." Looking down at her own slightly plump figure, she added, "It's too bad that's not my problem."

"I haven't had much time to eat lately," Laurel admitted. "It's been a busy week for me, too. Last night Joe and I worked half the night away trying to straighten out the newspaper budget."

"You need to hire some extra help."

"I can't unless they're willing to work for free." Laurel took another sip of her coffee. This had been a particularly rugged week. There was never enough time to get everything done on a small newspaper, especially with such a limited staff. Joe had to do all the advertising layouts himself, in addition to his duties as pressman. He even doubled as a reporter at times, going out to get a story if Laurel or one of the stringers didn't have time.

"Still having money problems?" Joan's voice was sympathetic.

Laurel nodded. "I'm hoping I'll have time to go over the budget this weekend. Joe is insisting that we add more advertising to increase our earnings, but I hate to give up any more of my news space."

"You always go out to that lighthouse when you've got something worrying you. It may have been a mixed blessing that the city allowed you access to the place."

Joan set down her mug and leaned forward intently. "You can't keep on running away forever, you know."

"What do you mean?" demanded Laurel.

"You spent all your free time there after Vince died. Your friends were hurt when you shut yourself away like that."

Laurel shifted uncomfortably in the chair, unwilling to admit that perhaps Joan was right. Sometimes being a newspaper editor was like living in a fishbowl. Because the readers of her weekly tended to view it with a proprietary interest, even Laurel's personal life was under the constant scrutiny of her neighbors. And although she cared deeply about her friends, she sometimes longed for more privacy, more freedom.

She knew that everyone assumed she had spent her days at the lighthouse grieving over her husband's death, and there was some truth in that. But in reality she'd known they never should have married in the first place. She had grieved over the useless loss of human life, but she knew her lover had died long before. The jealousy she should have felt over the other women in Vince's life had long since turned to simple humiliation.

Joan stood up and leaned over to pat Laurel on the shoulder. "I'm sorry. I didn't mean to interfere," she said anxiously. "Now I've ruined your weekend."

Laurel attempted a smile. After all, none of this was Joan's fault. "Don't be silly. Nothing could ruin this weekend for me. If you don't mind waiting a few minutes, I'll be happy to drive you home."

"Thanks, but I've got to hurry. Pete will be waiting for me." Joan trotted downstairs and pulled on her raincoat. "Say, Laurel, you wouldn't be interested in going out tonight, would you? You could call Howard . . ." Her voice trailed off as Laurel leaned over the banister and glared at her. "Okay, okay . . . I won't mention it again. Just don't blame me if you get lonely this weekend."

Laurel shrugged her shoulders and smiled. "Thanks, Joan, but no thanks."

With a cheerful farewell, Joan went out into the storm.

Laurel stood at the window after she left, gazing out at the empty streets. She hadn't seen Howard since last weekend. Somehow her encounter with that man at the club had left her dissatisfied with Howard, made her suddenly bored with him. Drew had been constantly in her thoughts since that night. There had been something about him, a compelling masculinity that had revealed a flaw in her own thinking about life. His blatant sexuality had reawakened emotions she'd thought were buried. She had imagined she was immune for life against that sort of sexual need, that raging fever that blinded one to reality, weakened one's resolve, made one lose control over oneself. The shield she wore held strong against most men, but she had to admit that for a moment that night she'd been tempted.

Fog was beginning to creep in over the coastline, making her realize she'd better get started. Maybe she'd be able to come up with a plan by Monday to prevent the sale of the lighthouse. There must be a way to stop that man. Already the lines of a new editorial were beginning to form in her mind. "J. A. Lockner," she whispered, "I haven't even begun to fight."

An hour later, Laurel slid behind the wheel of her small hatchback car, looking over her shoulder to make sure everything was in place. An ice chest, a bag of groceries, a small overnight case, a battery-powered portable radio, and a box of books and papers were jammed into the tiny rear of the car.

There was very little traffic on the road tonight, and soon she switched her lights to high-beam. Seeing the fog blankly reflect the brightness of her headlights, she instantly lowered them again, peering cautiously into the rain-soaked darkness ahead. At least she would probably have the beach to herself this weekend. No one else was likely to come out in this storm.

A streak of lightning ripped through the sky ahead of the car, almost blinding her with its intensity. The fog was getting thicker, no longer just patches of mist here and there along the road. Soon it was a complete blanket obscuring the landscape ahead. By the time she reached the turn-off to the lighthouse, her car was barely inching along.

Laurel's great-uncle had built this lighthouse about the same time her great-grandfather had founded the paper. In fact, *The Beacon* was named after that lifesaving light that had beamed out over the Atlantic Ocean on nights like tonight and kept ships from running aground on the sandy coast.

Her hands tightened on the steering wheel as she felt the tug of muddy sand against the tires. How awful if she got stuck at this point! She fumbled in the glove compartment and brought out a crumpled tissue, furiously wiping the inside of the windshield. It was futile; all the fogging was on the outside.

A sigh of relief escaped her lips as the comforting, solid bulk of the lighthouse loomed in front of her. She pulled the car as close as possible to the thick wooden door and left the headlights on while she dashed through the rain and battled with the padlock.

By the time she managed to swing the door open she was drenched. Setting down her purse inside the door, she hurried back to the car and got out a large flashlight before switching off the car lights. It took her three trips to get everything inside. As she ran back to shut the car doors, she was brought to a halt by a strange noise.

For a moment the only sound was the constant pattering of falling rain, but then she heard it again. It sounded as if someone was trying to get a car started, the whirring and groaning of a recalcitrant motor strangely eerie in the fog-shrouded darkness. After a while it stopped.

Laurel stood indecisively beside the door. Should she go and look for the car? Perhaps someone needed help. But if she drove off in this fog, she might not find her way back to the lighthouse before dawn. Another crack of thunder followed by a sharp increase in the pace of the falling rain settled the question. She would set the lantern by the window. Whoever was out there could find her.

Inside the lighthouse it was damp and clammy, musty from being closed up. Shining the flashlight ahead of her, Laurel made her way through the darkness to the center of the room until she found the edge of a table. It took only a second to light the kerosene lamp there, and before long she was able to see around the entire base of the tower. Nothing had changed since her last visit.

A damp chill seemed to permeate the entire room, and Laurel hurried over to the oil-burning stove on the far side. Luckily, she had restocked the supplies on her last visit, so there was plenty of fuel. Her wet clothes were sticking to her skin by the time she finished lighting the stove, but finally the room began to warm up. She dug a clean pair of jeans, a worn plaid shirt, and some fresh underwear out of her overnight case and hastened to the bathroom. Electricity had never made it out to the lighthouse, but the last caretaker had overseen the installation of plumbing.

She was just reaching for her clothes when someone pounded furiously on the outside door. She froze as a man's voice roared above the storm, "Damn it, let me in!" Her heart thumped uncomfortably, as her fingers fumbled desperately to pull on the filmy underthings. She fairly jumped into her jeans and shirt before running over to stand beside the door.

"Who's there?" Her voice came out thin and quavery.

The pounding continued. "Let me in! It's pouring buckets out here!"

Under any other circumstances Laurel wouldn't have hesitated a moment before opening the door. But with the storm raging outside and the shadowy darkness of the room behind her, it suddenly seemed as if tonight were a night for ghosts. She had grown up hearing stories about shipwrecked pirates and brigands, and her imagination was running wild, keeping pace with the symphony of thunder and lightning outside that door.

She became acutely aware of the fact that she was alone on a very isolated stretch of beach. She had a reason for being here, but why would anyone else be out in a storm like this? Unless he was up to no good...

The pounding stopped while she stood hesitating, to be replaced by a man's tired, pleading voice. "I just want to get in out of the storm. My car's broken down, and it's getting damned uncomfortable out here."

Laurel remembered the sound she'd heard earlier. Suddenly she felt like a fool. It took only seconds to fumble with the latch on the door and swing it open.

A man hurtled past her into the room. He could have been one of her ghostly pirates as he swept in, bringing a small part of the storm with him. Laurel flushed with a mixture of anger and embarrassment as his voice lashed out. "Don't just stand there. Get that door shut before it's wetter in here than it is outside!"

She grasped the door and moved to push it shut, but a sudden burst of wind flung the door back against her chest. The man moved past her quickly, ramming the door shut and flinging the bolt into place.

"Are you all right?" His voice was quieter, or did it just seem that way now that the storm was shut outside again? "That was quite a blow you took from the door."

Laurel was breathing raspily, stunned by the stinging force of the blow. "I'm fine," she finally managed to gasp.

"You don't look fine." She could feel him looking at her, but she couldn't yet meet his gaze. "Did I scare you? I'm sorry, but I wasn't sure anyone could hear me."

"That's perfectly all right. I'm fine now." For the first time she looked up at him. "You!" she gasped, letting her gaze trace over the dripping brown hair and rugged features.

His dark glance was appreciative, his eyes glinting at her in the dim light as he smiled. "It's a small world."

Laurel stared back at him, too surprised to speak. The last person she'd expected was this man. After their encounter at the club, she thought she'd never see him again.

"Maybe it's my lucky night after all." He eyed her slim figure speculatively. "I wondered when we'd meet again."

"Where in hell did you come from?" Laurel's comment was harsh, unfriendly.

"My car's broken down. Damn, was I glad when I saw your light!" Drew moved away from the door, gesturing toward the lantern.

"You're soaked." Laurel's voice was calmer now; she was in control of it again. "Come over where it's warm." She moved away from him, gesturing toward the pinpoint of light coming from the glowing stove.

She could see his shadow looming against the wall on her right side. Taking off his jacket and shaking it out, he already seemed to be relaxed and at home. When he didn't follow her, she turned back toward him. "Is something wrong?"

"Maybe I should take off these wet clothes. I hate to drip water across the whole floor."

Laurel stared at him for a moment. His corduroy jeans and flannel shirt were molded to his lean body, water running in little streams from the soggy fabric. "You have other clothes with you?"

"No, I was hoping you might have something around here."

"We're obviously not the same size," Laurel snapped.

"Obviously," he agreed, a smile lingering in his voice. "Perhaps one of your male friends has something I could borrow." Laurel lifted her eyebrows slightly, looking at him without speaking. "Surely you aren't staying out here alone?" His tone was slightly disbelieving.

He looked around the room, his intense gaze searching

the shadowy corners. For the first time Laurel had a chance to study his face. He was even more attractive than she remembered. His hair was sparkling darkly from the soaking he'd taken in the rain, and his mouth fascinated her, riveting her attention, her eyes tracing the frown that etched tiny lines from his firm lips.

"Just pitch me that blanket and I'll wrap it around me after I get out of these clothes."

For a moment Laurel didn't move. She didn't like the idea of his undressing. Even in his current rain-drenched condition he exuded a certain air of masculinity, a sexality that was somehow dangerous and threatening. She shook herself mentally; what was wrong with her tonight? It was ridiculous to be intimidated by this man.

She walked over and grabbed the blanket firmly, tossing it across the room. Immediately he was unbuttoning his shirt and unzipping his jeans. "Would you like something hot to drink?" she asked faintly, hurrying to the kitchen before he could answer.

Unpacking quickly, she put away most of her groceries and looked over the supply of battered tin plates and cups left from the days when she and her father spent most of their weekends down here. Her hands automatically went through the motions of filling the kettle with water and setting out a battered mug. Her thoughts were in a whirl that had nothing in common with her calm movements as she carried the kettle over to the hot stove.

He was there ahead of her, holding out his hands toward the warmth emanating from the fire. The blanket was wrapped around him toga-style, leaving his broad shoulders bare. His features could have been stamped on one of the Roman coins rumored to have been buried in the sands along with some unlucky ship. Heavens! What had gotten into her? First pirates and brigands, and now Romans.

He looked her over from head to toe, his gaze encompassing her bare feet and loose shirt. "Do you live here all the time?"

Laurel had no intention of filling this man in on the details of her life. "I'm here for a while," she hedged.

His gaze narrowed sharply. "Does the owner know you're here?" His question plainly implied he thought she might have broken into the place.

"The owner knows." She fixed her eyes firmly on a point just beyond his shoulder, her face carefully expressionless.

"Sure," he muttered, sliding his gaze along her slender body. "Does that radio work?" He changed the subject abruptly, pointing at the small portable sitting on the table.

For answer she flipped the switch and fiddled with the dials, stopping when she heard a man's voice issuing a storm warning.

They listened in silence to the report. Flash floods were expected throughout the night in all coastal regions, and the fog was making driving conditions extremely hazardous. His voice faded away, merging with the lively notes of a pop tune.

"Damn, this place is gloomy." Drew was gazing up into the shadowy shaft of the lighthouse tower, grimacing at the way the music was echoing starkly off the walls. The room was dominated by a central winding staircase that led to the top of the lighthouse. At the base of the tower the walls were at least twenty bricks thick, but they tapered off all the way up until reaching the top, where they were only three or four bricks thick.

Laurel was immediately on the defensive. "It may be gloomy, but it's saved the life of many a person on nights like this."

"But not any more. Now the ships are warned by radar and radio communications. These places are no longer useful." His words irritated Laurel beyond measure, and she was disgusted by the slanting gaze of his watching eyes.

She picked up the whistling kettle, wanting desperately to hurl its contents at him, but she restrained her impulse and poured the water into a mug instead. "Have some coffee," she said, seething anger apparent in her tone.

"Thanks." He grasped it eagerly, his fingers coming into contact with hers on the worn handle. "It looks as if you've got company for a while." A slight smile accompanied the words.

"What's wrong with your car?"

"I seem to have managed to get some water in my gas tank. A simple problem, really, but enough to get me stuck out here."

"You'll have to spend the night," she observed flatly, no welcome in her voice or expression.

"Women usually smile when they say that to me." His eyes seemed to be laughing at her over the rim of the mug as he took one last swallow before setting it down. "If you don't mind, I'll dry out my clothes over here by the stove. This blanket is a bit awkward, and something tells me you'd protest if I followed my natural urges and dispensed with the covering entirely."

He moved across the room easily, an athletic grace in his walk. Laurel went back to the kitchen, rage simmering inside her. Common courtesy demanded she offer him something if she herself were to eat, so she called out, "Have you had dinner?"

She was rummaging through the miscellaneous cans and boxes in the cabinets when he leaned around the partition. The blanket had slipped a few inches, revealing a tangled mat of curly hair on a hard-muscled chest. "I'm starved."

"Will soup and crackers be enough?" Laurel was already busy opening the lid of the soup can.

"I guess it'll have to be, seeing as you've already started preparing it." He was laughing openly now. "My, you are a bossy little thing, aren't you?"

She ignored him, trying not to rise to his bait. He was obviously arrogant, used to being able to charm women into submission. It was best to pretend she didn't notice.

As she poured the soup into a pot and added water, he reached around her, grasping the pot and moving off toward the stove with it before she could stop him. She gathered up crackers and fruit and followed him.

"How long has it been since you've eaten?" Drew asked, settling down on the floor while she perched on the edge of a wooden crate.

"Why?" she returned, the smell of the soup suddenly making her realize how ravenous she was. Her first mouthful of the hot tomato bisque made her wince.

"You look like you haven't had a meal since I last saw you. If I recall correctly, you attacked that food as if you were starving, too." He gave her a teasing smile.

She stared back at him without a hint of amusement. "Perhaps I'm just a compulsive eater."

He laughed, his dark eyes dancing. "Then you must have some secret. There's not a spare ounce on your bones."

"Thank you," Laurel said with false sweetness, finishing her soup without a pause and then selecting an orange to peel.

"What makes you think I meant that as a compliment? A woman needs a few curves."

Laurel raised her eyebrows. "I've seen the sort of woman you prefer."

"Don't worry," he said kindly. "Your curves are in all the right places." His eyes drifted over her lazily, sensually, appraisingly. A loud crash of thunder sounded as Laurel stared back, her mind hot and furious.

Suddenly she realized she was virtually at the mercy of this stranger. They were locked in together, prisoners of the storm raging outside. Laurel felt a quiver of uneasiness as she looked at him again. She was used to being in control of her own circumstances. Now she was at a loss about how to handle this situation. She glanced around the room. The comforting warmth of the stove had been invaded by a chilly surge. She had never wanted to be alone more than she did at this moment.

CHAPTER THREE

"WHAT'S UP THERE?" His husky tones broke the silence between them, dissolving some of the tension that had built in the last few moments.

She followed the direction of his gaze, staring into the darkness above them, tracing the faint outline of the circular staircase that led to the top of the lighthouse. "The staircase leads to the signal lamps."

"Is it still possible to climb all the way to the top?" he asked, moving over to stand near the base of the stairs.

"Of course. It hasn't been too many years since this lighthouse was in daily use."

"Let's go up now." It wasn't a request; it was an order. Even though Laurel felt a thrill of excitement when she thought of what the storm would be like from the top of the lighthouse, she inwardly balked at the command in his tones.

"Now?" she echoed.

"Scared?" He slanted an amused glance in her direction, his eyes silently daring her.

"Not at all," she answered coolly. "I just wanted to point out that you might find maneuvering the stairs a little difficult in that blanket."

"That's easily remedied." Even as he spoke, one lean muscular hand was whipping away the blanket, revealing far too much of his hard, muscular frame. Laurel turned away quickly, moving jerkily over to the stove and gathering up the remains of their makeshift meal. As she reached the kitchen she could hear faint sounds indicating that he was slipping on his jeans and shirt.

She lingered behind the partition as long as possible, unwilling to be close to him again. For some reason this man had the ability to get under her skin, to penetrate the wall of self-assurance and self-protection she had built over the past few years. Never had she imagined seeing him again, and certainly not under these circumstances. She resented her undeniable response to his magnetism, his unsettling effect on her senses.

This man bothered her. His steady, dark gaze seemed to see right past the unflappable, reserved woman who was Laurel Grey, editor of *The Beacon*. Those brown eyes flecked with golden lights under thick dark eyebrows seemed to contain a question she wasn't yet prepared to answer.

"You can come out now," he finally called.

Laurel deliberately turned on the water, rattling dishes loudly in the sink as she began to wash them in the icy flow. She mentally cursed her precipitousness, since she hadn't started the water heater yet.

She sensed Drew's presence the moment he walked up behind her, a sensual awareness that started her pulses racing and made her breathing slightly erratic.

Without saying anything, he rummaged around in several drawers before triumphantly producing a gaily colored towel and leaning against the counter near her. "Shall I dry?"

"Suit yourself," she answered shortly.

He picked up one of the bowls and polished it carefully, whistling cheerfully. She continued her savage attack on the dishes, eager now to get out of the tiny kitchen area, which seemed to be shrinking with every passing second. Even the harsh gushing of the cold water from the faucet as it struck the metal of the sink couldn't drown out his whistling.

She realized suddenly that it wasn't just an aimless tune. Her cheeks burned as she remembered the words to that song—"Strangers in the night . . ." As if reading her thoughts he began whistling even louder, and Laurel suddenly whisked the faucets shut and said roughly, "If you want to climb the stairs, we'd better start now."

"Do we use the lantern?" he asked. "Or do you have a flashlight?"

Laurel quickly produced her large flashlight in answer to his question.

The climb seemed endless, the beam from the flashlight bouncing off the rough walls on all sides of them as they slowly circled toward the top. Laurel was silent until they reached the tiny room that housed the signal lamps. From this height, the noise of the storm was close to deafening, streaks of lightning dramatically visible through the glass windows that ringed the room.

Laurel switched off the flashlight and stood near the window, her eyes adjusting to the blank darkness. Rain beat steadily against the glass, reverberating hollowly in the room. Usually you could see for miles from up there, but tonight there was only a black void outside the windows, lit occasionally by a flash of bright lightning.

She heard Drew moving about, his steps echoing on the wooden floor as he traced the lines of the round room. Strange, but his brief name seemed to match his personality. Abrupt, to the point, informal; he was all of those things and more.

What was he doing out here late on a Friday night? A dozen questions about his identity, his background, formed in her mind, but she refused to afford him the satisfaction of knowing she was interested. Probably he was expecting her to ask, thinking she'd be unable to control her curiosity.

Most women would find him very attractive, she acknowledged grudgingly. His face was not good-looking in an ordinary way, but it was strikingly masculine, and his smile carried with it a sort of careless confidence in his own sexuality, making her very conscious of the fact that he was male and she was female.

A sudden flash of lightning from beyond the windows revealed him standing very close to her, watching her with that same sharp, intense gaze that had unnerved her so when they'd met at the club. "Quite a place," he commented briefly, stepping back until his shoulders were resting against the large signal lamp in the center of the room. "How old is it?"

"The basic structure was built over a hundred years ago," she told him. "After the Civil War. A lot of the other lighthouses were damaged during the war, so this one was built to help out."

"You seem to know quite a bit about it."

"I've known it all my life. My great-uncle built this place, and his son was the caretaker after his father died."

"And you, are you taking care of it now?" Continuous lightning disclosed that his probing question was accompanied by a frankly sensual assessment of her slight figure.

Laurel bristled with irritation. Men were so obvious. Why was he unable to treat her like an ordinary person? Did the fact they were stranded out here together give him a right to turn this into a sexual battleground? Or did he treat every woman this way?

She kept her tones clipped and businesslike as she replied. "Unofficially, yes. I try to see that the building is kept up. Only a few lighthouses are left now on this part of the coast, and most of them are in danger of falling into the ocean."

"When was the last time this was used?" he asked, gesturing toward the signal lamp.

"About fifteen years ago. Then they built a Coast Guard station south of here and installed radar, so this place was closed."

"You still haven't told me whether you live here all the time," he prodded.

Laurel suddenly realized he was getting her whole life story, delivering his questions with a casual disinterest that managed to disarm her. "Does it matter?" she snapped.

"It might. Seeing as we're stuck out here, I wouldn't mind knowing whether you're stocked with food for a weekend or for a longer stay. After all, who knows how long the storm could last."

"What are you doing out here anyway?" Laurel could restrain the question no longer.

He lazily paced the floor, coming to stand right beside her. "I drove out here early this morning to do some sketching. Unfortunately I hadn't listened to the radio reports, so I didn't realize this storm was going to be anything more than a brief thundershower. By the time I hiked back to my car it was too late. The cap on my gas tank was loose, and enough water leaked in to keep me stranded out here."

So he was an artist. She should have thought of that. A lot of people in this area of the state came to the beaches to paint or sketch. He had a vaguely unhurried, rather nonchalant air about him that didn't fit in with a man who had a business to run. Funny, she hadn't thought that the first time they met. He was fairly young to be supporting himself by his artwork, though. Most young artists had to work at other jobs, fitting in their classes and artwork whenever they had some spare time.

It seemed he was moderately successful, too, or why else would he have been at Howard's little club? Although his clothes tonight were worn and a little faded, they were obviously of good quality, and the watch that gleamed on his wrist was an expensive model she'd seen advertised in a magazine.

She turned toward the window and leaned forward to rest her elbows on the ledge. "We could be cut off all weekend," she warned him. "Sometimes the tides during a storm completely cover the road from the main beach. That makes this little area of land more or less an island."

He came up directly behind her and placed his palms on the sill, one on either side of her. His chin rested on top of her head, his breath fanning her forehead. Laurel froze, her thoughts a whirl of confusion, his words barely penetrating the haze of anger clouding her mind.

"Which way is the road from here? I've lost my sense of direction." His voice was low and silken, the words seeming to convey some subtle message.

Laurel forced a reply from between her lips. "It's to our left, but there's no way of seeing it from here in this rain." He showed no signs of moving away from her, and her rage increased. She couldn't bear to feel trapped, especially by some man out to prove his masculine image. A sudden, unreasoning wave of fury swept over her and she whirled around angrily, arms flying out in all directions. Her right elbow struck the side of his jaw, catching him unaware and delivering a stinging blow.

Laurel stepped in the general direction of the stairs, dropping the flashlight when she bumped against a wall. Drew was still standing across the room, apparently stunned into a temporary silence.

The silence didn't last long. "My God, you little witch. What did you do that for?" His breath was coming in short, furious gasps.

She heard him groping about the floor, and then the flashlight beam switched on again, sweeping the room until it found her face.

"What was that for?" he demanded again, his voice firmer this time.

"You were crowding me," she answered harshly. "I was just moving away."

"Did you think I was going to attack you? There was no need to panic; I wasn't making a pass." His voice was dry again, full of mockery and a slight bitterness.

Crossing the room swiftly, he stopped right in front of her, sweeping the flashlight up and down her bedraggled figure with a calculated, insulting deliberation. "Maybe I shouldn't disappoint you; maybe you were hoping I *would* try something."

"Don't flatter yourself that I'd want anything from you. You're not my type." As she recovered her poise her voice was suddenly sharp and clear.

"You're not much yourself." He bit out the words with a savagery that shocked and angered her. "But I don't like being warned off before I've even thought of doing anything."

For a brief moment Laurel realized she could apologize. His face was probably going to be bruised, considering that her elbow was still aching where it had connected with his jaw. But his words had stung. She knew she wasn't looking particularly attractive, but she didn't need this arrogant male animal to point it out to her.

Her lips were moving before she could even think, the words tumbling out in an angry torrent. "Maybe we'd better get one thing straight if you're going to stay here for the night. I'm not looking for any sort of casual sexual encounter, and even if I were, I wouldn't be interested in a man so obviously aware of his own charms as you are. So just keep your hands to yourself and we'll get along fine."

The flashlight was thrown to the floor, and Laurel heard the sound of splintering glass a moment before her shoulders were grasped in a painful clench and she was jerked forward. His lips ground against her mouth, forcing it open and leaving her defenseless against the probing insistence of his tongue.

It wasn't a kiss, it was a deliberate insult; the controlled, savage mastery of his mouth said more clearly than words that he thought he could do whatever he pleased with her. She struggled against him futilely, trying to fight the arms that were tightening like bands of steel around her back.

Already weak from the rage she had felt moments

earlier and feeling faint under the relentless pressure of his attack, she suddenly went limp, her mind blanking out entirely for a moment. His clasp on her loosened when he sensed she had stopped struggling, his hold on her back slowly turning into a caress, his fingertips lightly tracing her spine.

Laurel seized the opportunity and shifted away quickly, bringing up her hands to push forcefully against his chest. Her shove caught him directly in the diaphragm, and he grunted, toppling back against the signal lamp and striking the side of his head.

His body crashed to the floor, and Laurel stopped her mad flight. She got down on her knees and felt around frantically for the flashlight, wincing as her fingers scraped across broken glass. Where was that light?

Dear God, what if she'd knocked him out, killed him even? She finally found the light and switched it on, breathing a sigh of relief when the beam came on as strong as ever. Hurrying across to where Drew sat slumped on the floor, she shone the light on his face and leaned over. Her fingers lightly skimmed his cheek, encountering a large bump below his eye.

"Damn! Get away from me, Laurel. You're dangerous!" His voice, remarkably, hadn't lost its cool, cutting quality, and Laurel felt almost sick with relief when she realized he was conscious.

Their eyes met and locked, both of them fighting for control against the emotions that had run wild moments before. "Are you always this violent?" he finally asked. "Or do I just bring out the worst in you?" He was, she realized with a sense of shock, laughing.

After looking at him in stunned silence, Laurel suddenly joined him, her own laughter bordering closely on tears. When she could finally catch her breath she said, "I thought I'd killed you."

"You might have at that," he muttered, cautiously moving his body away from the lamp and feeling his cheek with one firm, tanned hand.

"You're bleeding," she said, her voice shaking slightly. "We'd better go back downstairs. I've got a first-aid kit down there."

Pushing away her hand, he stood up. "I'm still just a little wary of having you near me," he laughed. "Have you taken a course in self-defense, or does this kind of behavior come naturally to you?"

Laurel felt herself flush a deep, dark red, grateful the light wasn't shining directly on her face. Of all the stupid, ridiculous situations to be in! He must think her a fool.

He was already walking down the steps, not waiting for her to follow. She hurried after him, and they moved quickly down the circular path without speaking.

Once downstairs, he went into the tiny bathroom, and she could hear water running in the sink as he splashed his face. Thank goodness she always kept a first-aid kit out here. She found the small case under the sink in the kitchen and brought it back out to the table, checking to see that the stove was still burning and turning up the lamp until it gleamed brightly.

He came out, drying his hands and face, to find her waiting by the stove. "I'm not going to apologize," she informed him defiantly, though she still felt a faint trace of worry. "You brought this on yourself, you know."

His eyes narrowed slightly, and she saw the cut on his cheek. "I'm not mortally wounded," he stated calmly. "I think we both need to do a little apologizing. If we continue behaving this way, one of us really will get hurt."

Hooking one foot under the rung of a chair, he dragged it over to the stove, still drying his hands as he spoke. "Let's get one thing straight right now. I'm not in the habit of molesting strange women. Sex is definitely more enjoyable if both partners are willing. So you can rest assured I'm not after your body, and you can quit jumping every time I come near you." He shrugged his shoulders and grinned wryly. "I guess I should be grateful I got off this lightly. Who knows what might have happened if you'd had a weapon!"

Laurel snapped open the first-aid kit sharply and pulled out a bottle of antiseptic solution. "Do you want me to take care of that cut?" she asked, keeping her voice steady and polite.

"Can I trust you not to come after me with the bandage scissors?" he asked lightly, a grin touching the corners of his mouth and making the golden flecks in his eyes more apparent.

It was impossible for her to maintain her aloof dignity in the face of his constant joking, and Laurel gave in gracefully. "You can't be sure, can you?" she said wryly.

She kept up a constant stream of light chatter as she carefully washed the cut with the antiseptic and applied a bandage. Drew lounged back in his chair while she worked, his dark gaze ruffling her composure as he studied her face. "That ought to take care of it," she said finally. "I promise I'll warn you if I feel like directing any more punches in your direction."

His hand shot out and wrapped lightly around her waist, drawing her down until she was level with his face. Looking directly into her eyes he said, "And I promise I'll warn you if I feel like kissing you again. Agreed?"

Laurel hesitated for a moment, a protest rising to her lips. Then, seeing the teasing glint in those mesmerizing eyes, she nodded.

CHAPTER FOUR

DREW SAT IN front of the stove, his long legs stretched out toward the warmth of the fire, while Laurel finished unpacking her box of groceries and straightened up the kitchen.

"You wouldn't happen to have an old raincoat around here, would you?" he asked when she came back. "Something about my size?"

"There's a locker in the kitchen," she answered. "You can rummage around and see what's left."

As she stared at him, a question lighting her eyes, he said, "I think I'll walk over to my car. I've got some gear I'd like to being in—some dry clothes and some books. Since I'd planned on staying with some friends this weekend, I do have a few things with me."

"Won't they be worried if you don't show up?"

"I imagine they'll decide the storm stopped me," he said blandly.

"So you're not actually from this area?" Laurel couldn't

help asking the question. She was beginning to get very curious about this man.

"I have a home near Wilmington, but I was invited to stay with friends for the weekend."

"And do some sketching," Laurel added for him.

"Yes, that too." He frowned. When he didn't elaborate, Laurel took the rebuff gracefully. No more questions, she told herself firmly.

When he came back from the kitchen he was holding a yellow slicker. "I'll be back in a few minutes," he said cheerfully, sliding the short parka over his muscular shoulders. It was far too small for him, the sleeves ending several inches short of his sinewy wrists with their fine sprinkling of hairs. Her gaze traveled slowly over the length of his corduroy-clad legs, noting the way the worn fabric molded his lean hips and firm thighs.

"Back soon," he murmured, and swinging open the large door, he disappeared into the storm.

After he left, Laurel sat down near the stove. Rainy weather always depressed people and made them behave oddly. It was something to do with the atmosphere, she remembered vaguely. Or perhaps it was just her tiredness. She'd been up late so many nights in the past few weeks her body was probably desperate for sleep. Leaning back in the chair, she closed her eyes and tried to relax.

Her mind conjured up a picture of the man who had just left. The effect he was having on her was disturbing. Nothing escaped his attention, and under his steady observation she was beginning to feel like a specimen pinned down for him to study.

What did he see when he looked at her? Judging from the way she'd been behaving, she wouldn't be surprised if he saw her as a snappish, bad-tempered man-hater.

Opening her eyes, she pulled restlessly at the faded fabric of her jeans. They were clean and neat, but it had been ages since she'd bought anything feminine or flattering to wear. Joan had been pointing that out to her for months now, suggesting they go on a shopping trip together, but Laurel always refused. Too busy, she excused herself. Maybe it was really that she didn't want to have to take a good look at herself and her life.

A long series of shattering thunderbolts brought Laurel back to the present with a start. She'd come out here to work on that editorial for the paper, and she'd better get started now!

She was sitting in front of the battered table, its surface littered with books, papers and back issues of *The Beacon,* when Drew returned.

He burst into the room, the yellow slicker dripping water and his thick brown hair soaked again. This time, though, he was carrying a small overnight case under one arm and a picnic hamper under the other. His jeans were dark from the hems to the knees, thoroughly soaked. "The water is starting to get deep in places," he explained when he saw her staring at his trousers. "It's still pouring out there, and I don't think it's going to let up any time soon."

He shed the jacket as he spoke and bent down to take off his shoes. "Any chance of getting a hot shower in this place?" he asked, a rueful grin creasing his face.

"Believe it or not, we have almost all the comforts of home at our disposal," Laurel said. "I'll see if I can get the water heater started up. It's an old gas model—runs on bottled fuel—and sometimes it's a little cranky about starting. If it works, there should be enough hot water for each of us to have a brief shower." She was moving toward the bathroom as she spoke.

"Perhaps we should conserve energy." Drew's voice came from right behind her as he followed her into the bathroom. "If we bathed together we'd each get a longer shower."

He grinned cheerfully as Laurel turned around indignantly, an angry retort trembling on her lips.

"Just joking, Laurel. It's obvious you're above such things."

Laurel jerked open the cabinet containing the water heater. This man's innuendos were getting a bit tiresome. Was the subject of sex always top priority, or did it just seem that way? Was that all he had on his mind, or was she taking everything he said too seriously?

"How about letting me do that," he offered as Laurel checked the pilot light and felt around in her pocket for a match.

"I'm perfectly capable of doing it myself, thank you," she retorted.

"Yes, I can see that. You don't need a man to do anything for you, do you?" Drew leaned lazily against the wall beside her, his slump bringing his face to the level of hers.

Her fingers trembled slightly as she lit the match and turned on the gas. Nothing happened. Laurel jiggled the handle on the gas line, frowning as she lit another match. "Having trouble?" Drew asked, the sardonic lift of his eyebrows irritating her beyond measure.

"If you'd move back a little bit it would help. You're blocking the light."

"That's right," he said pointedly. "It's always convenient to lash out at someone else when you're having difficulties."

"Oh, just shut up," she sputtered angrily. "If you want a shower you can light the damn heater yourself." She flung herself out of the bathroom and sat back down at the table, tapping a pencil angrily on its wooden surface.

Her teeth gritted with annoyance when she heard his lazy, aimless whistling directly behind her chair. She looked up to find him standing beside her, that cheerful grin back on his face. "It's lit," he announced confidently. "You didn't have the gas line open enough."

"Fine," she snapped. "You can have the first shower."

He pulled a packing crate over beside her chair and settled down on it, his long legs stretched out comfortably in front of him.

"Work!" he exclaimed. "This is Friday night. It's the weekend, you know. One should never work on a Friday night."

"If a job needs doing, there's no time like the present," Laurel quoted back at him, her voice assuming the inflection her father's had always had when he uttered that maxim to her.

"Oh, by all means, work must be done. But there has to be time for relaxation, too, you know." He consulted the gleaming watch on his arm, pushing back one damp shirt cuff and showing her the hour. "It's after ten. There's no point in working at this time of night."

Abruptly he stood up and reached for one of the newspapers. "Are you a reporter?" he asked. He flipped open the paper and searched out the masthead. "Laurel," he murmured, looking at the names. "L. Grey, Editor," he read out. His eyebrows rose in surprise. "Don't tell me you're L. Grey," he quizzed, eyeing her speculatively.

"And why not?" she asked.

"Well, for one thing you gave the name Ashley at the club—"

"That was my date's name," she interrupted none too politely.

"And somehow," he continued blandly, "just looking at this paper, I'd picture it being edited by a bald, slightly paunchy, self-important, middle-aged man," he told her. "Look at these stories." One long firm finger tapped impatiently on the paper. "Mrs. Jones of 128 Wynrock Road was a guest of the Peter Jones family at lunch on Sunday. Mamie Tate and her daughter went to Disney World last week and enjoyed a fine time." His tone disparaged the articles as he read the leads aloud.

"This happens to be a small-town newspaper," Laurel flared angrily. "We publish stories about what's happening to the people in our town. It's too bad you think it's funny, but to our readers these things are important." She jerked the paper away from him and glared furiously.

"You stay up late on Friday nights working on that sort of nonsense?" he said disbelievingly. "It's no wonder your stories are so boring. You're not doing anything worth writing about."

"At least I have a steady job," Laurel flashed. "I don't wander about the countryside drawing, and I don't find myself stranded on other people's doorsteps for the weekend."

Her jibe didn't even seem to faze him. Laughing lazily he sat down and leaned back again, locking his hands behind his head.

"How did you get to be editor of the newspaper?" he asked.

"My father was the editor. I took over after he died."
Her temper flared again as she saw a knowing gleam
enter his eyes. "That doesn't mean I don't know how to
do a good job," she insisted defiantly.

"Having a father in the business does help," he calmly
pointed out.

"Don't you ever work on a weekend?" she asked,
quickly changing the subject.

"Not if I can help it," he pronounced with obvious
self-satisfaction.

"What if something needs to be finished?"

"There's always something needing to be finished,"
he admitted reasonably. "That's the whole point. If you
don't decide to take some time off for yourself, you never
find time for having fun. It seems a bit silly to constantly
rush around working and to suddenly drop dead from a
heart attack before you've had a chance to enjoy living."

"Maybe work is the way some people enjoy living,"
Laurel suggested tentatively.

Drew's eyes narrowed, the dark brows slanted. "I've
found that most people who work nonstop are trying to
hide from something."

His remark hit too close to home, and Laurel cringed
inwardly. With a show of flippancy she said, "That sounds
like a lovely excuse for taking it easy."

His mouth twisted. "Not if your father died from overwork trying to satisfy a wife who wouldn't settle for less
than the moon."

Laurel stared helplessly at his disturbed expression,
unable to think of anything to say to soften the pain she
saw there. He shifted abruptly, the frown giving way to
his former amusement. "Anyway, that'll never be my
problem," he stated firmly.

"No overwork for you?" she inquired lightly, happy the awkward moment had passed. She didn't want to know too much about this man; every nerve ending in her body was already far too aware of him.

"Right," he affirmed. "It just so happens I can think of a lot of other ways to enjoy life besides working. It's possible to have it all—work and play. And play is definitely more fun!" He grinned at her wickedly, his eyes resting on the creamy shadows of her breasts faintly visible below the open collar of her shirt.

"I guess some men never grow up," Laurel said with a shrug of her shoulders. "Toys when they're young, women when they're older, but always playing."

"What makes you so sure I'm not a hard worker?" Drew asked sharply. "It isn't impossible for someone to work hard as well as play hard. If you know how to balance the two, you're much better off."

He leaned over closer to her and said, "You ought to try playing sometime, Laurel. It can be very enjoyable." He brushed one finger softly along the line of her jaw, his eyes seemingly fastened on the curve of her lips.

Laurel turned back to her work, and finally Drew moved away, searching through his bag before going into the bathroom. While he was showering, Laurel hunted up two sets of sheets and gathered up all the blankets. There were four bunks in all, two double sets. She debated for a moment before making up the two lower bunks. They'd just have to sleep near each other, there was no getting around it.

By the time he emerged from the shower, she was waiting outside the door, flannel pajamas and toothbrush in one hand, towel in the other. Sliding quickly past him, she escaped into the bathroom. The shower felt wonderful, the water hot enough to counteract the effects of the damp weather. She stayed under the stinging spray until it began to grow cold and then got out, towelling herself dry as quickly as possible and slipping into the flannel pajamas.

Peering into the mirror, she saw the steam had curled several escaped tendrils of hair around her face. The pajamas looked awful, but they were certainly modest enough, enabling her to appear in front of Drew without a robe. Bracing herself for his inevitable comments, she walked out into the main room.

He didn't need to say anything at all; his expressive dark eyes left no doubt of his disapproval. "I got a bunk ready for you," she told him, gesturing across the room. "There're plenty of blankets, so you should be warm enough."

Drew lifted his gaze from the book he was reading just long enough to acknowledge her comments. He was wearing only a pair of faded blue jeans; the lean, bronzed shoulders were bare, and so were his feet.

"I guess I'll go on to bed," Laurel said finally. "If you want to stay up for a while, go ahead. Be sure to put out the kerosene lamp before you go to sleep."

"Thanks," he murmured, surprising her by smiling briefly. "I really do appreciate your allowing me to stay here, Laurel. It's a lot more comfortable than my car."

He was devastating when he smiled, she acknowledged reluctantly. His smiles lit up every part of his face, the golden flecks glinting in his eyes, the little creases radiating from either side of his mouth. It took an effort for her to turn away and say good-night before sliding beneath her blankets.

* * *

It was pitch black when she opened her eyes. Pitch black and cold. Laurel lay still for a moment, not sure what had awakened her. A moment later she gave a stifled scream as something wet and decidedly cold touched her cheek. She sat up cautiously, mindful of the bunk above her, and traced one hand tentatively across her face.

Water was dripping from somewhere, she realized as another drop hit her, this time grazing her arm. She felt around cautiously, drawing back abruptly when she discovered the bricks of the wall next to her were completely slick.

The blankets had slipped away from her shoulders, and she began to shiver. The temperature must have dropped by at least twenty degrees, and combined with the water condensing off the old bricks, it was decidedly uncomfortable.

Her hands groped around the floor beside the bunk until they found the flashlight. Swinging gingerly out of bed, she winced as her bare feet hit the cold floor and padded quickly across to the stove. It had gone out, she discovered, feeling the stone-cold metal. A slight rustling behind her caused her to jump and spin around.

"Hey, it's only me," Drew joked softly, laughingly raising one arm in front of himself as if to ward her off.

"You startled me," she said.

"I'm not taking any chances. I remember what happened the last time I startled you."

The man was impossible! As her hand on the flashlight steadied, she was able to see him more clearly. His bronzed muscles gleamed in the hazy light, his body bare except for a pair of briefs that barely skimmed his hips. She looked back toward the stove quickly, strangely disturbed.

"The stove's gone out," she explained. "I'll have to light it again." She shivered slightly, this time unable to prevent the tremors that shook her slim frame.

"You get back into bed," he ordered, noting her shaking hands. "I'll take care of the stove."

"My bed's wet," she said flatly. "Water's started condensing on the inside of the bricks, and it's dripped all over my blankets."

"I've got the same problem," he admitted. "I suggest we drag our mattresses over here by the stove for the rest of the night."

While he lit the hurricane lamp and worked on the stove, she began gathering up dry blankets and pillows, moving them over to the floor near the one source of heat. She was tugging at one end of her mattress when firm fingers covered her hands. His clasp was strong and sure, his arms on either side of her, his warm breath fanning her cheek as he said, "Better let me help."

Laurel took a deep breath, fighting against her awareness of the closeness of his body against her back, the feel of his hands, the warm, dry scent of his skin. Twisting her head around slightly, she looked up to find his face only inches above her, his gaze tracing her lips with a look as intimate as a caress.

When he easily pried her fingers from the mattress and turned her around into his embrace, she made no protest. He continued his compelling study of her lips, and she moistened them slightly with the tip of her tongue. Her mouth was suddenly dry, her breath coming in shallow, erratic bursts.

"I promised to warn you if I felt like kissing you again." His voice was low, husky with an emotion she couldn't define. Just before his mouth covered hers, he whispered, "I'm warning you now."

The lips that touched hers were incredibly warm and seductive, urgently demanding her response. Nothing could have prevented her from yielding at that moment; no act of will could keep her from reveling in the feel of his lips moving against hers, his fingers softly massaging the curve of her neck, his body pressing so close to hers that she found it difficult to breathe.

She was no longer shivering from the cold; her body felt heated, a warm current pulsing through her in time with the quickening beat of her heart. His lips became more insistent, his tongue seeking to deepen the caress, and as Laurel wrapped her arms around his back, her fingers digging into the solid muscles, he lowered her gently to the bunk.

His lips left hers just long enough to rain brief, hot kisses along her slender neck, his tongue exploring the hollow at the base of her throat. A sigh escaped her as his kiss slid down to the soft swell of her breasts, his fingers swiftly unfastening the buttons of her pajama top.

"Laurel," he whispered, his breath warm against the curve of her breast. He was taking time to discover her as no man ever had, his heated hands caressing her body, exploring, arousing, teasing, awakening her. Her mind protested he was a stranger, a man she knew nothing about, but her body betrayed her, moving beneath him, delighting in the realization that she was invoking an answering arousal in him.

For a few moments she battled against the small, entreating voice telling her to push him away. She realized things were going too far; within moments she wouldn't be able to say no. Was that what she wanted? A night of passion in exchange for her self-respect? Suddenly recognizing how vulnerable she was to this man simultaneously frightened her, strengthened her weakening resolve and brought her back to the present with a start.

"Stop," she cried, rolling away from him, swinging so she could sit on the edge of the bunk. Pushing her tangled hair back from her face, she stared at him wordlessly for a moment.

"Laurel?" he questioned, moving to sit closer beside her.

"We'd better get back to bed," she said unevenly, gasping as she heard her own words. What if he thought she meant something else! A measure of sanity returned to her clouded mind, and along with it, some of her customary poise. "Let's just forget it," she said.

His gaze covered her face, his eyes taking stock of her in a disturbing manner. "I couldn't forget it," he solemnly assured her. "But I'll stop, if you'd prefer that."

Without answering, she straightened her top and moved across to the stove. It took only a few moments for him to maneuver the mattresses into position nearby, one on either side of the table.

"Thank you," Laurel said briefly. "And good-night." She threw her own blankets and pillow hastily onto her mattress and settled down noisily. Her body tensed as she waited. She was sure no man gave up that easily. Her mind was already forming the cool, clipped sentences she'd use to dampen his ardor.

"Good-night, Laurel, and thank *you*," he said silkily, a hint of laughter in his voice. She rolled over in surprise and watched as he doused the light, turned his back on her firmly, and was soon asleep.

* * *

When she half opened her eyes again it was morning. Squinting straight up to the top of the lighthouse, she could catch just the barest glimmer of light. Rain was still pelting against the building, not as spectacularly as last night, but in a continuous drone.

As the rest of her senses gradually awakened, she realized Drew was in the kitchen. An inviting whiff of frying bacon drifted across the room, and she wrinkled her nose appreciatively. How long it had been since she'd awakened to find someone else cooking breakfast!

She pulled the blankets up around her chin and snuggled down, contented to lie there, feeling strangely comfortable. Perhaps it wasn't so bad having company for the weekend.

As a faint whistling sound grew louder, Laurel opened her eyes again and glanced toward the kitchen, only to find Drew standing in the doorway, a huge red-and-white-checked apron tied around his waist.

She burst out laughing; she couldn't help it. He was grinning unabashedly. It seemed nothing could ruffle his self-confidence.

"You look ridiculous," she announced.

"Sorry, but this was the only thing I could find, and since I'm a little low on clothing this weekend, I decided to take care of what I've got on." He smiled at her appreciatively, his glance almost tactile as it slid over her tousled hair and sleepy face.

"Is that breakfast I smell?"

"Actually, it ought to be lunch," he retorted. "It's almost noon."

"Heavens, it can't be." Laurel sat up abruptly. "I never sleep until noon."

"There's a first time for everything," he answered

smoothly, his smile not quite reaching his eyes. As she stared back at him, his eyes narrowed a little, and she realized the top buttons of her pajama top had come unfastened. His eyes made a swift appraisal of the exposed flesh between her breasts before she clutched the shirt closed.

"How about breakfast in bed?" he suggested. "It's still chilly in here, so why not just stay there in front of the stove where it's a bit warmer?"

"That sounds terribly indulgent." She smiled. "What are we having?"

"You'll see soon enough. Judging from the rather unimaginative supplies I found in your kitchen, I think I've done fairly well in coming up with a fantastic breakfast," he bragged.

Rearranging the tumbled blankets around her, Laurel leaned back against her pillow and waited, listening to Drew moving about in the kitchen once more. He was obviously having no trouble finding his way around in there. Cabinets opened and closed, silverware clinked against dishes.

"Just about finished," he called. He emerged a moment later carrying a large tray from which a tempting aroma wafted. The apron was gone, and she saw he was wearing a pair of neatly pressed denim jeans and a dark blue plaid flannel shirt similar to the one he'd worn the night before. The shirt was open at the collar, leaving bare the tanned column of his neck and a small vee of his chest. A memory of how that chest had felt under her fingers the night before popped into her mind.

The tray was deposited on her lap with a flourish, and then Drew grabbed her pillow and arranged it behind her back. "Comfortable?" he asked. "This is a great meal; I want you to be able to fully appreciate it."

"It's fine," said Laurel. "Where's your breakfast?"

"Back in a second," he promised. Striding into the kitchen, he returned a moment later with another tray. She expected him to sit at the table, but instead he sat down on the floor beside her, his tray on his lap.

"Are you always in such high spirits in the morning?" she asked grouchily.

"Only when I have company," he said cheerfully.

"The blonde, or is it a different one every morning?" Laurel murmured, glaring at him.

"Being a bachelor has its advantages," he pointed out.

"Really?" Her eyebrows lifted.

"Never mind."

The food was wonderful. The bacon was exactly the way she liked it: hot, crispy, crunchy. It was accompanied by a perfect cheese omelet and squares of buttered toast. Laurel enjoyed every bite. "It's very good," she finally acknowledged.

"Good?" he argued. "It's great, and you know it!"

"You don't need me to feed your ego," she said with asperity.

"You'd be surprised. I'm really very susceptible to flattery."

"Especially from the female of the species?" she conjectured.

They continued the meal in silence, and then Drew looked up. "You haven't told me whether you're used to having company in the morning."

"A different man every morning," Laurel said flippantly.

"I suppose it's those blue flannel pajamas that draw

them." He grinned at her wickedly. "They're irresistible."

Laurel smiled without amusement, setting her tray aside. "I'm going to wash up and get dressed now."

In the bathroom, she peeled off the flannel pajamas and glared at them. Before she could analyze her reasons for doing so, she dumped them into the wastebasket.

CHAPTER FIVE

IT WAS SOME time before she emerged from the bathroom wearing her usual jeans and shirt. She'd done her best to make the outfit look better, tucking the shirt into the waistband and combing her hair carefully. Her long, thick lashes bore just a faint trace of mascara, and she'd highlighted her high cheekbones with a rosy blush that she knew flattered her fair skin.

Drew was waiting for her beside the staircase, reading one of her newspapers. "Let's go up to the top again," he suggested. "I'd like to see what it looks like in the daylight."

"Sure," she agreed, "but what about the dishes?"

"All taken care of," he said confidently. "I even un-packed my picnic hamper. We're in luck; I've got a bottle of wine I'd planned on giving those people I was sup-posed to visit this weekend."

He led the way upwards this time, taking the stairs at

such a pace she was fairly running to keep up. They reached the top in no time, drawn by the gray light filtering down from the huge windows above.

"Isn't it beautiful?" Laurel gasped when they stood at the top of the staircase. Waving one hand toward the panorama before them, she led the way across to the far window. Rain was beating against the glass steadily, but it was no longer threatening.

Instead, the view resembled a scene from an old black-and-white movie, a study in contrasts. The sky was dark gray, broken here and there by puffs of filmy white fog. Far below, the sea had taken a steely hue, the waves cresting in churning whitecaps before throwing themselves onto the rain-drenched sand. From time to time the screeching cry of a gull rose above the sound of the rain.

"When I was younger I used to come up here and imagine what it would be like to be out on that sea during a storm like this." Laurel's voice was hushed and low.

"With you all alone fighting against the elements?" he accurately surmised.

Laurel glanced up, expecting to see derision, and was confused by the look of tenderness she met. "I guess so," she said softly. "I spent a lot of time alone as a child."

"With a vivid imagination working overtime, I'll bet. Did you always daydream about the past?" His voice was husky, drawing Laurel into a circle of intimacy.

"I like history," she defended sharply, fighting to restore the more casual atmosphere she preferred. "Anything so terrible about that?"

"Maybe the past has been glamorized a bit too much. Those old sailing ships were pretty uncomfortable."

"Uncomfortable, yes, but wouldn't it be exciting to be tossing about on the sea, not knowing whether you were going to be dashed ashore by the next wave?"

"I'm not so sure how exciting the prospect of a watery grave is—under any circumstances. Anyway, thank goodness for radar. Now we can look back on the days when lighthouses were in use and see them as romantic and exciting. Back then, they were simply a matter of life and death. A lot of people were glad they're being replaced by something a little more dependable."

"How can you say that?" Laurel protested. "People love these lighthouses. They're symbols—"

"Of a past that's dead and gone," he broke in firmly.

"That's not true!"

Drew stared down at the sea, his face closed and hard. Laurel walked over beside him and leaned against the glass. "There are some people who'd agree with what you say," she told him, her eyes on the scene below. "But don't you see, these lighthouses are important. People lived in them, men survived because of them, fishermen depended for their living on the lighthouses to tell them when it was safe to go out to sea."

Drew turned and smiled at her. "Why do you love this place so much? You're too young to have memories of when it was used."

"My family built this lighthouse," she reminded him simply. "I've loved it all my life."

"It doesn't still belong to your family, does it?" he asked dubiously.

"Unfortunately, it doesn't." Laurel turned back to the window, concentrating on following the path of a swooping gull. "Several years ago my father donated the property to the city for a public park—with the provision that his family would always have access to the light-house."

"And what's wrong with that?" His eyebrows lifted in a quizzical frown.

"A huge development company is trying to buy the land. They want to build condominiums back on the main beach up there. That would block access to this land for public use, so they want to buy the lighthouse as well." She knew there was bitterness in her voice.

"You don't like the idea?" Drew leaned his back against the window, his arms crossed in front of him, watching her intently.

"I hate it!" Before he could say anything she continued, "It will ruin the lighthouse. The beach will be a commercial playground and—who knows?—they'll probably tear the building down eventually."

"It can't stand here forever," Drew murmured quietly. "It must take a lot of money to keep this place up."

"You sound just like the mayor." Laurel lifted her chin defiantly. "He says the town needs money for the schools and other public buildings. The town council is tired of using funds on historic projects while the modern buildings need repairs."

"You'd rather see the place left as it is, gradually decaying and falling apart?" Drew's voice was calm, unhurried, but she sensed he was interested in her answer.

"I want the National Park Service to take over, make it part of the National Seashore." Laurel was hesitant to mention her idea. It was her own personal dream, but most of her friends disagreed, saying the government would never pay the town as much money for the property as would a private corporation interested in a commercial venture.

Drew was silent for a long time, his thoughts seemingly far away. Finally he turned toward the window again. "I have to agree the view is fantastic from up here. I can see why you like it." He slanted a smile at her, his eyes seeming to share her enjoyment of the isolation and splendor below them.

They stayed a few more minutes, long enough for her to point out to Drew where the road was located. It was covered with water, their access to the main beach cut off completely.

"We seem destined to spend the weekend together," he said lightly as they walked downstairs. Laurel refused to acknowledge the mixed pleasure his words gave her.

By late afternoon Laurel was feeling restless. The day had gone slowly, the constant sound of rain beginning to elicit an answering pounding in her head.

They'd spent the past few hours sitting at the table, Drew reading a novel he'd brought from his car and Laurel working on her editorial. She felt a small surge of satisfaction as she gathered up her books. When the paper came out on Thursday she'd have a strong case against the Lockner Development Corporation.

"You're looking awfully determined about something." Drew was watching her, a small smile on his face.

"I'm feeling good because I finished my editorial for this week. It will certainly give Mr. Lockner something to think about!"

Drew carefully shut his book, murmuring, "Mr. Lockner?"

"J. A. Lockner of the Lockner Development Corporation. His company is the one trying to buy this land,"

Laurel explained. "He's an overbearing prig," she burst out suddenly, "and I despise him."

"You know him personally?" Drew's voice was calm, a faint smile on his face, as if he found her outburst slightly amusing.

"I know him as well as I want to know him." Laurel's voice was tight with feeling. "He's one of those people who think money can buy everything." Her tone loaded with emotion, she continued, "He's managed to take a small construction company and turn it into one of the largest corporations in this section of the country. Unfortunately, he doesn't seem to have any respect for the natural beauty of the land he destroys."

"Perhaps you should get to know him better," Drew said slowly. "You should always have firsthand knowledge about your enemies. That way you don't make a mistake about what you're up against."

"There's no chance of my knowing him better," Laurel said firmly. "Our paths will never cross—at least they'd better not!" She finished clearing her papers off the table and then smiled at him. "How about some dinner? I may not be able to equal your breakfast, but I'm a fair cook."

"May I help?" Drew laid his book on the table, his well-manicured fingers resting on the smooth wood. He has nice hands, Laurel thought irrelevantly, lean and strong, just like the rest of him.

"If you'd like," was her answer. "You did cook this morning, though, so you can consider yourself excused if you'd like to keep reading." In answer, he followed her to the kitchen after checking to see that the stove was heating properly. "There's your apron," she grinned, pointing at the red-checked garment he'd been wearing that morning. She sorted through the groceries, gasping when she felt his arms go around her from behind.

"You can have the apron," he whispered softly, wrapping its ties around her waist several times before tying the ends in a huge bow. "Your waist is small enough to fit right between my hands," he muttered as if amazed, reaching his fingers across her stomach to demonstrate. "Don't you get enough to eat?" he gently teased.

Laurel fought against the desire to lean into the solid chest behind her. Pulling herself away stiffly she said, "Speaking of eating, we'd better decide what we're having for dinner."

"We've got a bottle of wine," his husky voice murmured just above her left ear.

"How about grilled steak?" she countered. "I think this piece of meat will stretch to two portions, and we can make a salad to go with it."

"Are you always so practical?" His voice contained a mixture of resignation and amusement. Sliding his fingers lightly down her hips, he reluctantly let go of her.

Laurel unearthed a can of mushrooms and selected seasonings for the steak while Drew worked on the salad, whistling under his breath.

"You like music, don't you?" Laurel observed as they sat down to eat.

"Among other things," was his answer.

The gleam in his eyes made it clear what he was thinking, but Laurel feigned misunderstanding. "You're referring to your art? Is sketching your main interest?"

"I appreciate all forms of art." His eyes flicked over her. "The female form is symmetry at its best. Would you consider modeling?"

"No," snapped Laurel. "What type of artist are you, anyway?"

Drew chuckled. "Mainly a watercolorist. Seascapes are my favorite."

Laurel gave him an appraising glance. If Drew was able to support himself selling original watercolors, then he must be an exceptional artist, indeed. "I understand it takes a lot of talent to do that."

"Mostly hours of practice."

"Did you study art, or are you self-taught?"

"I've had some classes, but they were cut short—" He stopped abruptly. "Do you know much about the field?"

"Only as an art lover. I'd love to be able to afford some of the works I've seen, but I have to content myself with a few prints. Do you sell yours locally?"

A closed look came over Drew's face as he reached for the plate Laurel offered him. "Occasionally," he said.

In spite of the battered dishes and rustic surroundings, dinner couldn't have tasted better in the most elegant of restaurants. Drew, Laurel was rapidly discovering, was not only a very attractive man; he was also witty, intelligent, and charming. She found herself thinking illogically that no man could have fit more perfectly into the setting of her lighthouse. Already Drew seemed to belong here, his lean, broad shoulders and powerful, masculine body looking comfortable and natural.

Howard hated the lighthouse, she mused. The last time they'd brought a picnic lunch to the beach he'd spent the entire time complaining about sunburn and fussing over the way the wind kept blowing their paper plates along the sand. Vince's attitude had been no better. He'd refused to come unless they made a party out of it, inviting only friends of his, since he had little interest in anyone Laurel cared for.

Drew was a complete contrast. He was also dangerous, her instincts supplied. Dangerous because he made
her sharply aware of things that were missing from her
own life. Dangerous because his natural ease in these
surroundings was lulling her into thoughts she had no
business thinking.

Laurel lost count of the number of times Drew poured
wine into her glass, but by the end of the meal her mind
was decidedly hazy and she felt deliciously warm and
cozy.

The kerosene lamp cast a shadowy glow over Drew's
face, making his eyes seem darker than ever and emphasizing the planes of his face. They had been dis-
cussing a wide variety of subjects, finding they both read
voraciously, shared a love of Western art—especially
paintings by Russell and Remington—and enjoyed a
common passion for sailing and sailboats.

"Have you ever been in love?" Drew's voice slid the
question in casually, and Laurel had to think a moment
before she realized he'd changed the subject.

"In love?" she echoed faintly, tracing a pattern around
the edge of the table with her fingernail. "Isn't that a
rather personal question, coming from someone I barely
know?"

He shrugged his shoulders, watching her intently with
the merest suggestion of a smile.

"I thought I was once," she answered finally. "Was
I ever mistaken!" Without looking up she said, "And
you?" She was shocked to find she was holding her
breath, as if his answer held a sudden meaning for her.

His reply, when it came, infuriated her. "You're right,"
he said. "That *is* too personal a question to ask." With
a light chuckle he scraped his chair back and picked up

the dinner plates. "Shall we wash the dishes?"

Laurel followed him slowly into the kitchen. Why had he asked that question? Was he really interested in knowing more about her? He was a confusing man. In some ways he seemed instantly familiar, like someone she'd always known. At other times he was a total stranger, an enigma, an unknown quantity.

Was he in love with that blonde? Somehow she didn't think so. Of course she knew nothing about the other girl, but if her mind matched her appearance, her relationship with Drew probably had little to do with love, Laurel concluded with smug prejudice.

Pulling a fresh towel from a drawer she dried the dishes as Drew stacked them in the drainer. From time to time their eyes met, and once, as she reached for a plate, their hands touched. An electric shock flared through her, and she snatched her hand away as if she'd been burned.

At last there was nothing else to be done. The meal was completed, the table cleared, the dishes washed and put away. Laurel hesitated at the door of the kitchen as Drew cupped his hand over the top of the small kerosene lamp and gently blew it out. The lighthouse was almost totally dark except for the faint glow of light from the stove. An alarm went off in her head as she sensed his approach behind her.

She knew even before he reached her that he was going to kiss her. It was inevitable, as natural as the inexorable attraction between sea and shore. His arms slid around her body, pulling her back against him, his hands once more spanning her waist. He turned her into his arms, his lips seeking hers even as she moved her face upward to meet his.

His lips teased hers, moving away to press light butterfly caresses along the line of her jaw and the high bones of her cheeks, then returning to claim her mouth with a breathtaking passion. His strong hands slid down over her hips, pressing her closer to him, molding her body against him until she felt boneless and weak.

Of their own volition her hands moved to the back of his neck and her fingers tangled in his hair, drawing his head down with a restless, seeking motion. The sweet taste of the wine still lingered in his kiss, his tongue probing the moistness of her mouth. When his lips left hers she gave a soft moan of protest, which changed to a sigh of pleasure as he pushed open the collar of her shirt and trailed a line of fiery kisses along her shoulder.

With a gesture of impatience he pulled the ever-present barrette from her hair, twisting the long strands around his fingers and tugging gently until she leaned back to look up into his face. "I want to look at you, to touch you, to hold you," he whispered huskily, his gaze almost burning her with its intensity.

After that there was no more time for words. His fingers unwound themselves from her hair and moved urgently over her body, burning through the thin cotton material of her shirt, tugging it loose from the waistband of her jeans. His lips brushed her hair, her mouth, her throat, shooting flames of sensation through her fevered body.

She was scarcely aware of the moment when her shirt slid to the floor and his hands began to move with velvet smoothness over the bare skin of her back. Her fingers fumbled with the buttons of his shirt, seeking the wiry mat of hair on his hard, muscled chest, the smooth firmness of his back.

Her bra fell away with a soft whisper of the sheer fabric, allowing his insistent, demanding hands full access to the curves of her breasts. A blind need for fulfillment soared through her as his deep, smooth voice crooned his desire. Again and again he kissed her, the almost punishing pressure of his hard mouth against her lips slowly changing into a deep tender caress that threatened to drive her wild. He became a gentle, unhurried lover, the touch of his hands a tribute, as if there was nothing else in the world more important than this time, this place, this woman in his arms.

Without the slightest appearance of effort, he lifted her in his arms, carrying her until he could gently deposit her on the blankets before the stove, whose glow echoed the white heat of her building passion.

His body moved to partially cover hers, his lips renewing the soul-discovering kiss of a moment before. Desire consumed her as his hands continued their slow exploration of her body, his fingertips tracing ever-narrowing circles around the swell of her breasts. His tongue soon greeted their rosy tips, teasing them to firmness and setting off currents of dizzying delight.

His fingers tugged at the waistband of her jeans, releasing the snap and zipper and sliding them from her body with one swift motion. Laurel was beyond thought, beyond reason. She was lost in a kaleidoscopic swirl of the present, reveling in his tender orchestration of her senses. The warm, intimate scent of his skin filled her nostrils, her ears rang with his short, broken, husky breathing, and she thrilled to the silken sensation of skin against skin.

"Laurel," he breathed, his breath warm against her

breasts. The sound of her name on his lips had a sudden, shatteringly sobering effect. What was she doing here, lying naked with a strange man, surrendering to his passionate embraces? She didn't even know his last name. She knew almost nothing about him! Was she going to let another man gain control over her so easily?

It must have been the wine, she told herself desperately. Why else would she lose all grip on her sanity like this? With no further thought she pushed at him, shoving him away from her, sobbing, "No, no, get away from me."

He moved away instantly, leaving her shivering and trembling. The faint glow from the stove behind him cast his bare shoulders and face into shadow, making it impossible for her to read his expression.

"The wine," she mumbled hastily. "It went to my head."

Drew's voice was harsh and thick. "What the hell do you mean?"

Laurel grabbed one of the blankets, pulling it over her body with quaking fingers, sitting up slowly. "I'm sorry, truly sorry," she began again.

"Don't," he said angrily. "Forget the excuses." Holding himself rigidly away from her he bit out, "Let's get one thing straight. Up until two seconds ago every cell in your body was screaming yes."

"I must have been crazy," she muttered fiercely.

"You're crazy if you think you can say no to me at this point!"

"Can't control yourself?" she flung out bitterly. "Isn't that every man's excuse?"

With an obvious effort at that very control, Drew

shrugged his shoulders and twisted his lips in an attempt at a smile. "If you want to stop, we'll stop. That's *all* there is to it."

Surprised by his answer, she stared at him for a minute and then grabbed her clothes. Clutching the blanket around her nakedness she fled into the bathroom. Cool water splashed on her face helped to restore her calm, but her reflection in the mottled mirror did nothing to restore her confidence. Shadowed eyes, tangled hair, and a con-fused, distraught expression were what she saw.

After running her fingers through her hair, she thought for a moment, then disconsolately fished her pajamas from the wastebasket into which she'd so cavalierly tossed them that morning. What could she have been thinking! She shivered in disgust, donned the flannels, and wrapped the blanket around herself again. Without a backward glance in the mirror she returned to the main room.

Drew was already lying on his own mattress, seem-ingly engrossed in his novel. Crossing quickly to her bed, Laurel managed to slide under the covers without making much noise. When Drew didn't speak she called out softly, "Good-night."

"Good-night," he said without looking up. After a moment's silence he added, "You don't mind if I have the lamp on for a while? I'd like to read."

"Of course not," she said stiffly.

"Good-night, then." His voice was calm and unper-turbed. She looked at him suspiciously. Not one trace of the feeling she'd seen earlier was left in his impassive features. Hadn't it affected him at all? Wasn't he even a little upset that she'd said no?

In her experience, dominant men were unable to ac-cept failure; some primitive instinct drove them to control, to win. Why, then, was Drew so calm? Was this an act, a mask he wore to cover his real anger?

Laurel turned over and pulled the blanket over her shoulders, lost in thought. Obviously his emotions hadn't been involved. Otherwise, how could he look so calm when she was left so ragged and uncertain? Irrationally she found herself thinking that he could at least look disappointed. It was the very least he could do.

CHAPTER SIX

THE MINUTE LAUREL opened her eyes Sunday morning she knew something was different. She lay still for a moment, listening intently. It was quiet in the lighthouse, totally silent.

It wasn't raining anymore! The constant, drumming sound of pelting raindrops was gone and her ears almost rang with the silence.

She stretched luxuriously, enjoying the sheer delight of lying there relaxed and warm under a pile of blankets. With a sudden rush of remembrance her peaceful state was banished. Last night! How could she have forgotten? And how was she going to face Drew this morning? He'd been so remote, so cold as they were settling down for the night. In fact, he'd fallen asleep before she had, his calm, quiet breathing almost driving her insane as she lay awake suffering waves of confusion.

She felt a flush of anger. It wasn't her fault, she told herself furiously. He'd had no right to expect her to fall into bed with him. She didn't need to help him prove anything about his masculinity.

What irritated her the most, though, was that he hadn't seemed disappointed at all. Apparently he hadn't really cared whether she shared his bed or not. The passionate prelude to lovemaking that had left her confused and filled with longing hadn't affected him in the same manner at all. Her own emotional reaction was humiliating when contrasted with his cool acceptance. Maybe this was just a male tactic she hadn't encountered before; a new maneuver in the chase-and-retreat style of mating.

She felt a sudden urge to be alone, away from the lighthouse, away from Drew. As quietly as possible she slipped from beneath the blankets, and tiptoed across to the bathroom, stopping only long enough to grab a pair of beige corduroy jeans and a soft, fluffy knit top in a warm terra cotta shade.

Once dressed, she brushed her thick hair briskly and, for once, left it free of the tight barrette. She combed it down over her shoulders, letting it curl softly around her face.

Tiptoeing back across the room, she paused and looked at Drew. He was still sound asleep, his lustrous brown hair slightly rumpled on the pillow. The blankets had slipped down to his waist, exposing his deep bronze chest with a mat of sun-gilded hair gleaming against the white of the sheets.

Reluctantly tearing away her gaze, she slipped back the bolt and swung the door open cautiously, breathing a sigh of relief once she was outside. A gasp of delight escaped her lips as she surveyed the scene in front of the lighthouse. Gone were the dark clouds that had obscured the sky for the past two days. Gone, too, were the slanting rain and murky fog.

Clean white sand sparkled in front of her, reaching down to a spectacularly blue expanse of water capped with white-crested waves. As she watched, two stately blue herons swooped down to the beach in front of her and stood looking at the sea, seemingly as absorbed by the view as she was. Farther away several sandpipers darted here and there along the water's edge, joined by an occasional seagull.

The air had a salty, crisp bite to it, and a steady breeze whipped tendrils of hair across her face. The beach had the pristine, untouched look that always followed in the wake of a storm, the white sand marked only by an occasional mass of tangled seaweed or an ornate collection of shells tossed up from the depths of the ocean.

Although the air was still slightly chilly, the sun was already peeking over the horizon. Laurel kicked off her shoes with a laugh and started running toward the water, enjoying the sense of freedom and solitude.

She reached the snow fencing that formed a barrier near the end of the sandbar and looked for the road. Shielding her eyes with one hand she stared across the broad expanse of sand. Yes, there it was, way off in the distance, a bare glimmer of asphalt visible between the scruffy pines. But she could see a wide band of still water near the strip of beach that curved around to the little peninsula where the lighthouse stood. So they were still cut off. From past experience she knew it would be hours before the water retreated enough for a car to drive safely across.

She and Drew would have to put up with each other's

company—however awkwardly—for the rest of the day
at least. Perhaps by tonight they could leave. Oddly
enough, she didn't feel the surge of relief she should
have at that thought.

Turning back toward the water, she crossed her arms
across her breasts and stared blankly at the rolling sea.
She found it almost impossible to analyze her feelings,
to understand how Drew could inspire in her such a
confused, unsettled welter of emotions.

Slowly retracing her steps along the beach, she stopped
occasionally to examine a shell or pick up a piece of
driftwood. Tiring of this aimless occupation, she dropped
down to sit cross-legged on the sand, lifting her gaze to
the cresting waves. Her mind was filled with images of
Drew, her thoughts turning inexorably to the memory of
his lips against hers, his eyes sparkling, his hands sliding
firmly across the soft flesh of her breasts. What was it
about him that held her fascinated, lost in a spell of
captivated attraction?

Her response the night before frightened her, left her
confused. Never since Vince had she allowed any man
to get so close to her, never allowed any other man the
total access to her body that she had given so freely to
Drew. Why did he have this effect on her? Why was she
drawn to him like a moth to a flame? His kiss had the
power to reach her innermost recesses, freeing emotions
she'd hoped were buried forever.

Was it only because they were isolated here together,
cut off from the rest of the world? No, she admitted
unwillingly; despite his arrogance, she'd been aware of
her attraction to him that night at the club. Would she
be drawn to him wherever they met, whether alone or
in the midst of a crowd of people?

The door of the lighthouse slammed shut with a resounding thud, and she looked up to see Drew striding across the sand toward her, his hands thrust deep in the pockets of corduroy jeans, his powerful legs quickly shortening the distance between them. The breeze was whipping his shirt back against his body, outlining the powerful muscles of his chest, baring the strong column of his throat.

Laurel felt a surge of emotion she couldn't define as she studied his approach. Her gaze drifted across the smooth planes of his face and down the tapering lines of his torso and muscular legs. A wave of uncontrollable longing assailed her as he came up beside her, making her voice husky with feeling as she greeted him.

"Good morning," he answered, swinging his lean frame down to drop to the sand, sitting so close her shoulder was wedged firmly against his. "Sleep well?" His bland expression revealed nothing of what he might be thinking. His jawline was smooth and taut, freshly shaven, and his hair had been slightly mussed by the wind.

Laurel found it difficult to answer, her fingers tracing a nervous path in the sand as she looked away from him. "About last night—" she began hesitantly.

"Forget last night," Drew said abruptly. "Let's begin again." This time he gave her a slow smile, the friendliness back in his eyes, his mouth lifting slightly at the corners.

Laurel's heart was beating with an irregular rhythm, so loud she was sure he must hear it. "Fine," she agreed, smiling back.

"Quite a change from the storm," Drew commented with a gesture toward the calm, unruffled beach before them. The sun had risen above the horizon, glittering dramatically across the cerulean blue of the ocean. The breeze was warming swiftly, promising a hot, clear day.

"It's always beautiful after a storm," she responded thoughtfully. "The rain seems to wash away all traces of civilization, and you can almost imagine that this little area of the world has looked exactly like this for hundreds of years."

"Except for the lighthouse," his voice teased lightly.

"That's beautiful, too," she shot back defiantly.

"Not as beautiful as you."

Stunned by his words and unable to withstand the purposeful intensity of his glance, she quickly stood up. It wasn't fear making her breathing erratic and her pulse uneven, she knew. Neither was it uncertainty or confusion. With a flash of startling clarity she recognized her attraction to this man for what it was. Quickly, inevitably, she knew she was in danger of falling in love with him.

When he stood up beside her she didn't move. The nearness of his body was almost an embrace, yet he didn't attempt to touch her. Instead, he looked at her for a long moment and then held out his hand.

"How about coming back to the lighthouse for some breakfast?" he asked softly. After a moment's hesitation she put her hand in his, reveling in the possessiveness of his clasp as his strong fingers closed over hers.

They prepared breakfast together, sharing bacon and eggs at the table in front of the stove. Afterwards they cleaned the little kitchen in record time, both of them eager to be back out on the sunny beach. Finally they were strolling along the sand again, laughing at the antics of a lone, lazy turtle who had been lured from his hiding place out into the warm sun.

"How about a swim?" Drew suddenly suggested.

Funny how his eyes crinkled up at the corners when he smiled, Laurel thought idly as she stared at him. She'd never noticed that before.

"Well?" He was watching her intently, a questioning look crossing his face when she didn't answer.

"Now?"

"Why not?" He grinned at her. "The water looks wonderful, and the waves are fantastic. Don't you like to swim?"

"I love it. Unfortunately, I didn't bring a swimsuit with me this weekend. It was raining so hard, and I had so much work to do, I didn't think there'd be a chance."

"Who needs a swimsuit?" He grinned at her devilishly.

Laurel studied him for a moment. "I know there's not a great deal of difference between my underwear and my bikini," she said, "but really, I don't think—"

"Why wear anything?" he asked in a puzzled voice, a perfectly serious look on his face now.

"Sorry, it's against city ordinances to go swimming in the nude here."

Drew was already shaking his head. "Do you always play by the rules? Don't you know there's something basic and elemental about water and bare skin? They go together like a bear and honey, like pigs and mud, like—"

"Stop," she laughed before he could continue. "That's not the same thing at all."

"Why not?" He shrugged his shoulders lightly and made a face. "Just because somewhere along the line people started putting barriers between themselves and nature, it shouldn't prevent you from enjoying something as fun as swimming in the nude."

He grasped her chin firmly, his eyes glinting down at

her. "It's something you shouldn't miss. I promise to behave."

With a resurgence of the recklessness that had been rising in her all morning, she suddenly agreed. Why not? Why deny herself the pleasure? After all, what was she risking? Except maybe a little sunburn in a few places unused to the sun, she reminded herself ruefully.

"I'll race you into the water," called Drew, already shedding his shirt as he strode across the sand to the edge of the water. He reached for the zipper on his trousers, and Laurel turned her back to him.

A feeling of rashness assailed her as she heard him splashing into the water, and soon she had lightheartedly dropped her jeans and top to the sand. Her fingers hesitated only momentarily before she stripped off her brief nylon panties and bra. With a muttered, "It's now or never, Laurel Grey," she raced to the water and plunged in.

"It's freezing," she shrieked.

"You'll warm up soon."

Laurel raised her dripping head from the surf and pushed back her hair, turning to find Drew standing only a few feet away. His chest was gleaming, the sunlight glinting off the hairs on his chest, giving an impression of newly minted bronze coins. Her eyes watched in fascination as a rivulet of water traced its way down through the tangled hairs and trickled across his flat stomach.

The waves barely skimmed his slim, muscular hips, and Laurel realized with a little shock that when the wave had gone its way, the water level would be considerably lower.

How did one go about discreetly swimming in the

nude? she suddenly wondered. After all, if she floated on her back, too much of her front would be revealed, and if she swam, that would expose her whole backside to the surface of the water. Unable to come to a decision, she turned her back toward the shore, maneuvering herself carefully to insure that everything below her shoulders stayed beneath the water.

"Don't be so modest." Drew's soft comment was accompanied by a chuckle that made the hairs on the back of Laurel's neck stand up in protest. She could see the sardonic cast of his features right now, the insolent smile curving his lips.

In a gesture of defiance she raised one arm swiftly through the water, splashing Drew thoroughly, and then took off swimming away from the beach with a fast racing stroke. She was an accomplished swimmer and soon was far from shore. Pausing for a moment to rest, she looked back and saw Drew waving. The roar of the waves kept her from hearing what he said, but she could tell she'd surprised him.

He was right: Swimming in the nude was entirely different from swimming with even the briefest of bikinis. Silkily, sensually, the gentle waves caressed her nakedness, invoking a rapport between her senses and the elemental forces of nature. Luxuriating in the feel of the water, Laurel was content to drift for a while, lifting her face to the sun and soaking up its warmth.

An angry shout caught her attention. Drew was swimming toward her at a rapid pace. Treading water, she waited for him to reach her side, a curious breathlessness coming over her.

"You're out too far," he shouted angrily. "Don't you

know that after a storm you have to watch out for rip tides? You could be carried right out to sea by a strong current."

Without answering, Laurel struck out toward shore. She *had* forgotten; in her enjoyment of the feel of the water and the sun, she'd not been watching how far from shore she'd gone.

A slight splashing beside her indicated Drew had caught up with her. They swam side by side toward the sand until Laurel stopped and stood. The water here was getting too shallow.

"Nice, isn't it?" Drew panted. He was so close she could almost feel the presence of his body through the water.

They looked at each other for a long, wordless moment, and then his head came down swiftly, blocking out the sun. Laurel gave a brief gasp before his mouth captured hers. She drifted helplessly toward him in the water as he began to kiss her, trembling when her body met his expanse of muscled flesh, her breasts barely grazing his chest, her thighs sliding against his.

Purposefully, inexorably, his lips possessed hers, covering her soft mouth, drawing out a response she was incapable of denying. A small quiver shuddered through her as her lips parted slightly and she felt his tongue slip in and trace the inside of them. Lightly, gently, it caressed her mouth, so fleetingly only the slight taste of salt it left behind gave proof of its existence.

With a sigh she surrendered her mouth, opening it like a flower beneath his warm lips. His kiss tasted of salt and the sea, and as it deepened the waves took a part in their passion, moving her against him, twining their legs together, moving them apart and then together again.

Following a course as old as the tides, Laurel slowly and gradually moved from being a recipient of a kiss to being a full participant. Her fingers tangled themselves in Drew's hair, her body arched against his.

A sudden wave caught them unawares, knocking them over and washing them up with the tide, the pounding of the surf mingling with the drumming of her heart. Lying in the churning shallow water, Laurel reveled in the feel of his body, returning kiss for kiss, caress for caress.

At last their mouths broke apart and they lay winded, both of them breathing with difficulty. Drew was on his back, one arm holding her firmly against him, his eyes darkening as he obviously fought for control.

Stroking one hand lightly along her spine, he whispered, "I promised not to take advantage of you if we went swimming, but you're so tempting, Laurel. I want to make love to you."

At the directness of his statement she came to her senses. Without answering, she pulled herself swiftly from his arms, quickly struggled to her feet, and ran lightly across the sand to where her clothes lay, stopping only long enough to slip on her jeans and top. She stumbled off down the beach again. She had to get away from that burning look in his eyes, the expert hands that made her melt into his arms, aching for fulfillment. He offered her nothing but desire; he saw her as a conquest. If she gave in, she would lose control, make herself vulnerable to his desires. It was only an affair to him, a weekend affair that meant nothing, and she was a fool if she tried to make it into something more. She turned around once and saw him, now fully clothed, heading for the lighthouse.

By the time she returned, her nervous energy spent, he was mercifully gone. She settled down to try to work on the newspaper budget. Several hours went by, and she braced herself for some expression of his anger. She knew she was acting unfairly; their lovemaking was as much her fault as his, and she had no right to give in to her passion and then change her mind without warning. He would be an exceptional man indeed if he ignored her irresponsible actions for a second time with no words of reproof.

In the middle of the day she fixed herself a sandwich and wandered out to the beach munching on it, trying not to glance in the direction where she saw Drew seated with a sketch pad before him.

She needn't have worried; he was totally engrossed in his work. Exactly like Vince, she decided angrily, kicking a shell away with an impatient jab. How could men view women only as objects to be seduced, without realizing the emotions they stirred? Once Drew's ardor had cooled he had dismissed her without a thought, concentrating on something he considered more important.

Now she had to face a long evening, pretending that nothing had happened between them, that no sparks had ignited, that no embers were left smoldering, ready to burst into flames again.

"Has that shell done anything to make you hate it?"

Laurel turned at the sound of Drew's voice close behind her. One look at the dark frown on his face and she knew he had not been as nonchalant about their encounter as she had imagined. "Maybe it's myself I'm angry with," she said with a soft sigh. "Are you waiting for an apology?" She didn't intend to grovel; he was guilty, too. But she supposed the sooner they got over the awkwardness between them, the better it would be all around.

He grinned, chasing away his look of displeasure. "Unrequited passion always leaves me starving." As Laurel's eyebrows rose he added, "For food, that is."

She shrugged, feeling thoroughly put in her place. "I left sandwich makings in the kitchen."

"I'll settle for an apple. How would you like a clambake tonight?"

Laurel's eyes sparkled. "I'd love it. Low tide should be in an hour or two."

Late afternoon found Laurel and Drew on the beach searching carefully in the sand along the waterline for elusive clams. From time to time one of them would give a triumphant shout when the sticks they were using as spades turned up one of the plump, slightly oval ridged shells.

They had spent a long time searching for firewood, using small pieces of driftwood and finding dead branches fallen from some of the scraggly trees near the lighthouse. Most of the wood was too soaked to use, but eventually they'd collected enough to cook their dinner.

Choosing a spot sheltered behind a large sand dune to build the fire, they rolled down an old log to serve as a barrier. Drew managed to get the fire going while Laurel watched and offered an occasional piece of advice.

"Maybe you should do this yourself," he said at one point, an exasperated smile lighting his rugged features.

"Oh, no," she protested laughingly. "It's far too much

fun watching you have a go at it."

He made a face at her and turned back to his task, breathing a sigh of relief when a small spiral of smoke began curling up from the twigs at his feet.

By the time they finished collecting and rinsing the clams, the fire had become a bed of hotly glowing embers, perfect for the clambake they planned.

"What else shall we cook?" Laurel stood back from the fire and smiled up at Drew, pushing her tumbled hair back from her face. Her jeans were rolled up around her knees, her shoes discarded during the hunt for the clams. She was suddenly inordinately glad she'd brought one blousy, feminine top along with her usual flannel shirts. Its creamy color and texture, along with the covered buttons that opened into a gentle vee partway down the front, made her feel a bit more dressed up for their impromptu feast. "Shall we bake potatoes?" she suggested. "We can wrap them in foil and cook them in the fire. They'll taste wonderful."

"It sounds great," he agreed, matching his stride to her shorter one as they walked toward the lighthouse. Once inside, they gathered up plates and silverware, piling everything into Drew's picnic hamper.

The sun was drifting toward the horizon by the time they returned to the beach, the fire glowing hot and bright. Their spot behind the dunes was protected from the light breezes playing across the surface of the sea.

Drew set to work digging a cooking pit for the clams, then lined it with rocks he'd made sizzling hot in the fire earlier. Laurel watched in fascination as he added a bed of glowing coals, using a large shell to scoop them into the pit.

Looking up to find her watching, he explained, "We'll

bury the clams between layers of wet seaweed, then pack sand and more hot stones over the top." He was layering in the seaweed as he spoke, spreading the clams over the wet green strands. While he finished burying the clams, Laurel wrapped the potatoes in foil and pushed them into the fire with a stick.

After another long walk along the beach, this time in the faint, shadowy haze of dusk, they returned to the fire. Drew carefully unearthed the clams, pronouncing them fully cooked, while Laurel rolled the potatoes out of the fire and tested them for doneness.

The clams had opened during the steaming process, the insides of the shells glowing with a dusky pink crystalline sheen, the clams themselves tender and moist. Drew arranged them on two plates while Laurel melted butter in a small pot over the fire and unwrapped the potatoes. She poured coffee from the thermos into mugs, and they finally settled down to eat.

"I guess there's no graceful way to eat clams," Laurel laughed, her hands poised above one of the shells.

"That's why you eat them on a beach." Drew grinned at her, dipping a clam in the warm butter and offering it to her.

The meal was worth the wait, Laurel decided. She couldn't remember when anything had tasted so good. Perhaps it was the salty night breeze, perhaps it was the mysterious twilight around them, perhaps it was the man across from her who made everything a delight, a new experience.

"That was heavenly," Laurel sighed with satisfaction before stacking their dishes in a neat pile at the end of the log. By the time they settled back on the blankets the moon was glowing above them, a bright crescent of light in the dark sky. Drew leaned back beside her, resting his weight on his elbows, his long legs stretched out comfortably toward the fire.

A light breeze ruffled Laurel's hair, tossing a few strands across her cheeks and eyes. Looking over at Drew, she found he was staring at the sky, watching the first few faint stars beginning to appear in the dark blue expanse above them.

She knew nothing about this man, really, and yet it seemed she knew the important things. He seemed to have a basic honesty, a simplicity that embraced life to the fullest, stripping away the nonessentials and reaching to the very depths of her heart. Did she dare trust her own instincts about him? After all, she had been fooled by a man before—a man very much like this one in certain ways.

"Why so serious?" Drew's fingers moved lightly along the line of her jaw, and she turned her face into his palm, her eyes meeting his quizzical, smiling gaze.

"It's so peaceful out here," she whispered. "The sea, the sky, the whole world, as if we're the only two people left in it."

"We're the only two people who matter." Drew's fingers tightened on her chin, his other arm reaching around her suddenly, pulling her in one swift motion against the long, warm length of his body.

Their lips met in an endless moment of time, a swirling, dizzying, passionate moment whose ending was foretold before it even began. His mouth claimed hers with unabashed possessiveness. Tasting the sweet surrender of her lips, his tongue met hers with a fiery demand that left her breathless and shaken.

She gave a convulsive shudder and lifted her slender

arms to his hard body as his hands roamed intimately over her back, her ribcage, the soft sides of her breasts. His lips moved leisurely to explore her face, sliding down to the throbbing pulse at the base of her throat until they found the hollow between her breasts, then returned to reclaim her mouth. If she had ever thought of resisting, she now knew it was hopeless. His expert hands and lips were sending her to higher and higher levels of ecstasy until her aching body demanded release.

They moved as one to lie down on the blanket-covered sand, his fingers gently massaging the sensitive cords of her neck as he shifted his body, positioning her beneath him. His fingers slid with rough insistence under the soft fabric of her blouse, his lips leaving hers only long enough for him to slip the garment and her bra from her, push them away, and capture her breasts in his large hands.

As the cool breeze struck her heated body, her fingers fumbled with the buttons on his shirt, seeking the hard warmth of his broad chest. A small sigh of satisfaction escaped her lips as her fingers found and kneaded the rippling muscles of his back. At the same moment she felt the touch of his bare chest against her tingling breasts.

His lips covered her throat and shoulders with fleeting kisses and then trailed down to her soft, creamy breasts, the slow, sensual, yet insistent darting and gliding of his tongue driving her crazy with desire. Even as her fingers tightened on his shoulders, pulling him closer against her, he breathed her name softly.

"You're beautiful, Laurel. Kiss me again," he whispered hoarsely. His breath fanned her nipples as he lifted his head slightly and gazed into her eyes. After that his movements became gentle and unhurried, only the heated urgency of his breathing and the pounding of his heart against her sensitive breasts revealing that his need was as desperate as hers.

They moved together, skin against skin, mouth against mouth, their legs entwined. Some part of her mind said she ought to stop. Yet even as she thought it, she knew with sudden clarity that she wasn't going to push him away again. She wouldn't, she couldn't, she'd die if she did.

Her hands, guided by the passion invoked by his love-making, slowly traced the pattern of his body, helping him remove the last barriers of clothing between them.

Then he was beside her again, his fingers playing her senses with the skilled orchestration of an artist. Her eyes sought out the bared masculine hardness of his body, her hands following the path of her rapt gaze. With a muffled groan he pulled her against him, his body poised over hers, his voice, husky with passion, murmuring her name over and over as their bodies merged in a slow, sweet, inevitable act of mutual possession.

With a burst of flame the storm inside them raged out of control, thunder crashing and lightning flaring, a spiraling tempest of fevered desire, cresting on a tidal wave of endless, burning ecstasy.

For long, incalculable moments she lay in Drew's arms, her head cradled on his shoulder, their bodies clinging in the warm aftermath of love. "Now I know you're a dream." Drew's voice was low and shaky, his breath silky and soft against her forehead.

His fingers played along her spine, brushing her smooth velvety skin with feathery strokes. Laurel turned her face into his shoulder, her lips brushing the moist, heated skin in a tender, seeking movement.

They lay entwined on the blanket, reluctant to move

even an inch apart, unwilling to break the spell and leave the dream. The breeze off the ocean had freshened, a salty, chilly gust that cooled their flushed bodies. Drew pulled the blanket around them, turning her more closely into his arms, his breathing slowing to an even tempo that soon told her he was asleep.

CHAPTER SEVEN

THE LONELY CRY of a seagull overhead woke her up. Laurel lay silently for a moment, still and confused. Her dazed eyes took in the sight of what seemed to be millions of stars twinkling above her in a midnight black sky.

A dull roaring sound gradually identified itself to her mind as the pounding of waves on the shore. Her body registered the fact that another body was entwined with hers, a weight pressing gently against her breasts. She turned her head slightly, letting her gaze travel over smooth shoulders, powerful neck, and the tangled thick dark hair that outlined Drew's sleeping face.

She didn't remember falling asleep. She had no concept of how much time had passed. Drew's arm lay possessively across her breasts, his lean, muscular legs partially covered her own soft thighs. She was filled with a strange tenderness, a desire to run her hands softly over that smooth back, snuggle closer into his protective embrace.

Nothing in her life had prepared her for the total peace, the sense of completion she was experiencing now. This man had reached into her life, touched something deep inside her, possessed her.

Possessed her! She felt the sense of total peace and satisfaction ebb away as surely as the tide from the shore below her. How could she have responded to Drew with such mindless abandon? Who was he? What was he? Why, she knew almost nothing about him! She sat bolt upright, gasping as Drew shifted his position, breathing a sigh of relief when he didn't awaken.

She needed time to think, time to consider this turn of events. Her clothes were still lying on the sand beside her, and she groped for them quickly, shivering as the breeze grazed her bare shoulders.

She couldn't think clearly. She knew only a sense of desperation. She had to get away, away from this man who so completely controlled her senses and mastered her body. Slowly, gently, so as not to awaken him, she slid on her jeans and flung her shirt over her shoulders, running lightly over the sand until she reached a bank of sea oats floating eerily in the moonlit darkness. She paused briefly, taking one last look at the man still sleeping on the beach.

His arms were curved around the spot where she'd been lying; he was unaware as yet that she was gone. In the drifting light of the moon she could distinguish the thickly curving arch of his eyebrows, the arrogant line of his nose, his firm, compelling lips. A sudden longing assailed her, a desire to run back to him, to forget everything else and experience again the devastating demands of his passion.

Firmly, deliberately, she turned her back and hurried

on to the lighthouse. Inside, she wasted no time swiftly gathering up her clothes and restoring order to her appearance. The mirror drew her attention for a moment. Did she imagine it, or did her face look different? Softer, fuller, fulfilled?

Haste made her hands shake slightly as she packed up the books and papers she'd brought with her on Friday. Was it just two days ago? Two days since this madness had overtaken her?

She carried the box and overnight case out to the car, carefully opening the door and sliding them inside. Everything else could wait. She'd just have to trust him to lock up the lighthouse, to make sure the stove was out.

Trust him. That was ironic. She bit her lip in confusion. It was exactly because she didn't trust him that she was running away. A situation like this didn't fit into her plans at all.

This man was too dominating, too sure of himself. Sexual relationships clouded one's ability to see life clearly; in fact, they made one exhibit all the characteristics of an addict. And addictions invariably carried a price tag. The price of love was control, and she wasn't willing to pay it again, to give any man that sort of power over her.

A flutter of panic ran through her as she started the car. What if he heard her, tried to stop her? But nothing of the sort happened. The pounding of the surf effectively silenced the noise of the engine, and as she looked in her rearview mirror, her last sight was of the lighthouse standing tall and stark against the sky, a lonely sentinel— as lonely as she was going to be from now on.

Only a few inches of water remained covering the

road, and Laurel maneuvered her small car onto the main beach with no difficulty. The drive away from the shore passed in a haze. At one point she turned on the radio, searching the dials desperately until a disc jocky told her it was exactly half-past two on Monday morning. Had they slept that long? She'd had no concept of the passage of time.

Her mind was clearing now, a sort of dazed sense of reality telling her she'd been a fool. She hated herself, hated her body's traitorous response to Drew's love-making.

On the whole long road back to town she didn't pass a single car. The headlights cut a lonely swathe through the darkness ahead, illuminating the seemingly endless ribbon of black asphalt.

By the time she guided her car into the narrow alley behind the newspaper building and unlocked the back door that led to the apartment above, she was exhausted.

Both hands of the clock were pointing at three when she finally stretched out on her bed and tried to sleep. She was home now, safe from her own human frailty. She had won—or had she? The taste of victory was like ashes in her mouth.

In her determination to escape male domination, to maintain her independence, she had forgotten her own emotional needs. Drew had resurrected long-buried feelings, revealing a void, a dreadful, empty aching inside that left her tormented with doubts.

Pressing her face into her pillow, Laurel dissolved into tears, sobbing helplessly, crying out of a sense of loneliness and loss even as she cursed her own weakness.

Sleep was elusive, and by five she was up again, showering quickly and pulling on a dark blue skirt and delicate white silk blouse. She left her hair falling softly over her shoulders and after running a comb through it one last time, she descended the stairs to the office.

For the next two hours she worked relentlessly, going over the plans for the next issue of the paper, typing a clear copy of the editorial she'd written on Saturday. Work was the only reality, the only stability in her life, and she clung to it as if she were drowning.

Her fingers moved briskly over the keys, her brain refusing to let herself remember how Drew had looked, how he'd smiled, how it had felt to be in his arms. Forget him, her mind said. You'll never forget him, her heart warned.

Sudden relief flooded through her when she heard Joe's key clicking in the lock and looked up to watch her short, kindly pressman enter the office. "Good morning," he greeted her, looking a little surprised. "You're up early today, or am I late?" He looked absentmindedly at his watch.

"You're on time," she assured him with a laugh. "Come on in. How about some coffee?" It was a comfort to have company after the past few lonely hours, a relief to slip back into the familiar routine of her life.

"I'd love some." Joe's gaze darkened as he watched her carefully. "Something the matter, Laurel?"

She shrugged. "Nothing out of the ordinary. Why?"

"Those dark circles under your eyes, for one thing." He chuckled slightly. "If I didn't know you better, I'd think you'd been crying."

Laurel managed an answering smile. "You know better than that, Joe. But maybe I'd better get to bed a little earlier tonight."

Joe gave a satisfied nod, picked up a mug of coffee,

and went over to his desk to start his work. By ten that morning Laurel was feeling better. She and Joe had checked the wire service stories, searching for items of interest to their readers, and discussed her editorial. Joe supported her stand on the lighthouse, but he seemed to believe she didn't have a chance of winning. Nonetheless, he promised to talk it up to as many people as he could.

When the phone at Laurel's elbow rang, she picked it up and answered with a calm hello.

"Hi, there." Joan's good-natured voice came clearly over the line. "I've got more news for you about the lighthouse. How about meeting me for lunch?"

"Sure. Where?" Laurel agreed.

"Why don't you come over to my house?" Joan suggested. "Dad won't be home for lunch today, so we'll have plenty of time to talk. I can make something low-calorie. Too much high living over the weekend," she laughed.

You can say that again, Laurel agreed silently, even as she promised to meet Joan at twelve-thirty. Before long she was propping the small "Out to Lunch" sign in the window and closing the door of the office behind her. They always closed the office during lunch; Joe went home to eat, and the part-time helpers left at noon. On an impulse she unlocked the door again and scrawled a quick note for Joe: she'd be taking the afternoon off.

It was a short walk to the rambling old white house where Joan lived with her father. Theirs was one of the oldest houses in town, the original frame having been built in 1835. A widow's walk was perched on top of the roof, a reminder of the days when lonely wives spent their time watching for their husbands' ships to return.

Joan opened the door just as Laurel was reaching for

the bell. "Hurry up," she said impatiently. "I've got to tell you what's been happening this morning."

Her friend's urgency was a sure clue that she'd keep Laurel dangling until the proper dramatic moment. Laurel followed her back to the bright, sunny kitchen, idly wondering how long she'd have to wait for Joan to drop a bombshell this time. She patiently sat down at the round, solid oak table set with yellow gingham mats and snowy white china.

"We're having stir-fried chicken and vegetables," Joan explained as she combined her ingredients, characteristically postponing delivering her urgent "news." "It's supposed to be low in calories, but it tastes too good to be diet food."

Tasting the mixture of sliced vegetables and gently cooked meat a few minutes later, Laurel was inclined to agree. Poor Joan; she was always having to fight a slight weight problem, unlike Laurel, who never seemed to gain an ounce.

"So, what's been happening?" Laurel asked lightly, attempting to hasten Joan's revelation and to ward off any possibility of Joan's asking her about her weekend. They knew each other too well for Laurel to be able to hide anything once Joan got a whiff of it.

"James Lockner was in the office this morning!" Joan paused for a moment, waiting for the reaction that usually followed when Laurel heard his name. This time Laurel had trouble forcing herself to act interested. Right now the last thing she wanted to think about was the fight over the land. It only brought back painful memories of the lighthouse, the weekend, and Drew.

"Don't you want to know what he's like?" Joan asked, waiting expectantly.

"Of course," Laurel agreed hastily.

"He's devastating!" Joan told her breathlessly. Laurel's eyes narrowed slightly. She and Joan seldom agreed on their definitions of a handsome man.

"Oh, well, there's no use telling you about him," Joan said crossly. "Anyway, you'll be seeing him for yourself on Thursday. The mayor has called a town meeting to discuss the land sale, and Mr. Lockner's agreed to be there."

Now Laurel was decidedly more interested. Maybe she would finally get a chance to present her arguments in person to the Lockner Development Corporation.

"Thursday," she said thoughtfully. "The paper comes out that day, and I've written up our side of the debate in the editorial. That'll give everyone something to think about before they get to the meeting."

"I thought you'd like to know," Joan said smugly. Glancing down at her watch she gulped the last few bites of her lunch and stood up, apologizing. "I've got to hurry back. Mayor Boggs will be on the warpath if he doesn't find me sitting dutifully behind my little desk." As Laurel started to get up Joan waved her back down. "Go ahead and take your time. Finish your lunch. Just leave your dish in the sink and slam the door behind you." With a cheerful good-bye she hurried out of the house.

Laurel sat at the table a long time, her thoughts revolving in endless circles. She felt a need to get away from home for a while, to forget everything behind her. Maybe an afternoon in Wilmington would take her mind off Drew. She could be there in an hour. With a burst of determination, she stood up and prepared to leave.

She took the coast road as she left town. On the outskirts of the city she passed the turn-off to a new block of condominiums. "Shore Acres," a large sign proclaimed. "Owned and developed by the Lockner Development Corporation." Her hands tightened on the wheel. Until now she hadn't really focused on the meeting set for Thursday night. But it was something to think about, something to work for, something to make her forget.

With a renewed sense of purpose she drove down to the old Cotton Exchange, which now housed a myriad of small boutiques and shops. For a few minutes she walked around looking in windows, considering the garments on display. She really should buy something new for herself. She tended to select classic styles, mainly separates that could be interchanged and rearranged to extend her wardrobe. Most of the newspaper's profits were plowed back each month, leaving her only a small personal allowance. Until now she hadn't really cared; she had little time for social interests outside her work.

She broke off her musings when a strikingly fashioned turquoise silk dress caught her attention. It was stunning: a rich, elegant shade of blue reminiscent of the color of the sea on a bright, cloudless day. The dress had a deeply vee'd bodice supported at the shoulders by thin straps. A sheer jacket, demurely simple with a white lace collar, could be worn over the dress, making it useful for a wide variety of occasions. She entered the shop quickly before she could change her mind about splurging.

Two salesgirls came forward at once, and before long Laurel was in the dressing room, eyeing her reflection in a three-way mirror.

The dress fit her perfectly, the slim straps highlighting the golden tan of her shoulders, the rich turquoise providing a stunning contrast with her chestnut brown hair and deep blue eyes. One of the girls brought in a pair of strappy silver sandals, and Laurel slipped them on, pleased with the way they enhanced her shapely legs.

"How about this dress as well?" The other girl was holding out a soft, knit T-shirt dress in a delicious shade of coral. Laurel took off the silk dress and slipped the coral knit over her shoulders. The color was perfect, adding a soft, warm glow to her complexion. The delicate fabric outlined her slim figure, clinging softly and revealing the curves of her breasts and hips. "I'll take both of them," she announced firmly with sudden reckless-ness.

Buying the two dresses seemed to start a small land-slide. In the next two hours Laurel purchased two silky blouses in brilliant hues and added a slim gray skirt to her swiftly growing pile of packages. She hesitated only momentarily outside the windows of a lingerie shop be-fore going inside and buying a long silky nightgown in the same warm shade as her knit dress. The gown was slim and slinky with skinny shoulder straps that criss-crossed down the back to a softly plunging curve.

One thing was certain, she told herself as she came out of the shop. After this weekend, no matter what happened, she'd never put on a pair of flannel pajamas again!

Laurel had started down the broad, red brick steps that led to the street when she paused to glance around at the day. Standing in the shadows under a large oak tree she saw a dark profile.

Her mouth suddenly went cotton-dry, and she felt her pulse race wildly. The lean, muscular body, the broad shoulders, the thick brown hair were all exactly like Drew's.

She started forward impulsively, drawn magnetically by an urgent longing, his name on the tip of her tongue, her feet barely touching the ground. Her heart was threatening to leap into her throat as she pushed past several shoppers, frightened she might lose sight of him.

She was almost at the bottom level when he was momentarily blotted from her view. She then saw that a vaguely familiar woman, whose piled blonde hair and close-fitting dress made a bright splash of color in the gathering dusk, stood beside him.

April. The woman she had seen Drew with at the club. Their heads were close together, and Laurel was near enough to hear a husky laugh escape his lips.

In a blind panic she turned, colliding with a middle-aged woman who muttered something about rudeness to the man beside her. Laurel threw an apologetic glance over her shoulder as she hurried back up the steps, praying that Drew had not seen her.

When she reached one of the tiny restaurants on the upper level she sank into the nearest empty chair and ordered coffee. Only when the hot liquid had eased her inner shivering did she admit to herself how much she had longed to see Drew, to hear him speak her name, to feel his touch.

The incredible passion they had shared came back in a rush, and she had to fight to keep from screaming. Why, she asked herself bitterly, hadn't she stayed at the lighthouse and talked out her feelings with Drew? She could have asked him for time, for space, to catch her breath and sort out her feelings.

When the waiter glared at her sharply she realized she had been sitting over her cup of coffee far too long. Gathering up her various bags and parcels, she paid her check and left the restaurant. Once outside, she looked ahead carefully to make sure she didn't run into Drew and April. They were gone, of course.

It was dark by the time she got back home. She made herself a small salad and carried it on a tray into the living room, sitting in front of the window to eat, staring out toward the street.

Drew, she cried silently. Do you miss me at all? What did you think when you woke up and found me gone? Did you feel as empty as I do now?

She took her half-eaten salad back to the kitchen, disposed of its remains, and as she'd promised Joe, began preparing to get to bed early. She slipped into her new nightgown, brushing her hair smoothly down around her shoulders. A flicker of hope rose in her; perhaps everything was not as bleak as she was painting it, perhaps they would meet again. She wasn't ready to try to seek him out; her own feelings were too confused. But after this lighthouse fight, after the town meeting, maybe then she'd have time to sort her jumbled thoughts. She turned down the covers and climbed into bed.

As she drifted off to sleep, the memory of Drew's passion drummed through her veins, pounding in her pulse, promising fulfillment and an end to the aching longings of her body.

CHAPTER EIGHT

LAUREL OVERSLEPT THE next morning, waking only when she heard Joe entering the office downstairs and the loud clatter of the press as he began work. She hurried out of bed, trotting into the kitchen to make coffee. Sunlight was streaking into the small apartment, promising a bright day ahead.

A cool shower erased the last vestiges of sleep from her mind, and by the time she had dressed in her new gray skirt and silky rose blouse, she was wide awake. Running a brush through her newly washed hair, she stood for a moment at the window, watching the street below. For a moment a picture of Drew as she had seen him yesterday afternoon flashed into her mind, and she felt a surge of pain.

Would the memories ever fade, would her inner life and routine ever settle back to normal? Probably not, she admitted silently. Whether she liked it or not, the shell of ice that had encased her heart since Vince's betrayal had shattered into a million pieces, leaving her emotions vulnerable once more.

Joe looked up sharply when she came downstairs. His shrewd, friendly glance registered the shining hair and the new clothes. After a brief silence he said gruffly, "I was beginning to get worried about you. Thought maybe you were sick."

"No, I just overslept," she explained apologetically.

"You need to take a vacation, young lady." Joe's usually placid face was frowning. "It wouldn't do you any harm to be looking around for an assistant, either."

Laurel walked over beside him, watching as his deft fingers experimented with the layout of a new advertisement. "Dad always ran the paper by himself," she protested.

Joe looked over the top of his wire-rimmed glasses and glared at her. "Once your mother died your father lived for this paper. I don't want to see you do that. You're an attractive young woman with your whole life ahead of you. If Howard bores you, why not find some other nice young man and start having some fun?"

"Joe," Laurel objected, inwardly stunned at his perceptiveness about Howard, "you're an incurable romantic. Just because you and Cora have been happily married since high school doesn't mean it works that way for everyone. I found myself a 'nice young man' once, remember? I don't need another one of those. I like my life exactly the way it is." Even as she said the words, an inner voice was chiding her for the lie. She did want a man. Not just any man—she wanted Drew.

Joe glared at her again, his glance plainly saying he didn't believe a word of her protests. She smiled and sat down at her desk. The phone rang. "*The Beacon*," Laurel answered.

A grumpy male voice growled over the line, "My

name is Evan Brown. I renewed my subscription, and then the paper stopped arriving."

"Just one moment. I'll check." Laurel smiled over at Joe resignedly as she thumbed through the subscription file. Leslie, the high school student who handled their circulation department, had her own unique system of filing. It took Laurel several moments to solve the problem. Picking up the phone again she said, "I'm sorry, terribly sorry. We have another Brown on our list, and his name was right next to yours. It seems we extended his subscription instead of yours."

"As long as I get this week's paper, it's okay," the man warned before hanging up abruptly.

Laurel slowly replaced the receiver. It was going to be one of those days. Well, at least it might push aside her moody thoughts.

She and Joe were busy at the back of the office solving a mix-up in the classified department when the front door swung open and a middle-aged woman came in wringing her hands nervously.

"What can we do for you, Mrs. Baysdon?" Laurel asked, a friendly smile on her face as she pointed to the chair beside her desk. "Would you like a cup of coffee?"

The woman shook her head and, with trembling lips, launched into her tale of woe. "It's about my son. You know Bobby is a good boy, Laurel."

"Of course I do," she replied smoothly.

A smile of relief creased Mrs. Baysdon's face. "Then you won't put his name in the paper? I told Henry we could count on you."

Laurel pressed her lips together. "What's Bobby done?" she asked. A recurring problem in a small town was being asked by friends to suppress unfavorable news.

"He and some of his friends from school were a little wild on the beach last Saturday." The nervous frown was back on the older woman's face. "But he wasn't drunk!"

"We have to publish all arrests and court cases except of minors," Laurel said gently, "but if he's innocent, there's no problem." The poor woman seemed to think something this minor was the end of the world.

Mrs. Baysdon began dabbing at her eyes with a crumpled tissue. "Your father would have understood, Laurel . . ."

Laurel looked at her levelly, trying to keep the sympathy she felt from expressing itself in her voice. "My father always insisted on treating everyone equally. I'm awfully sorry, but we'll have to publish all the names. It's always been our policy."

After Mrs. Baysdon left, Laurel felt like a criminal. Sometimes she wondered why anyone was fool enough to stay in the newspaper business. Her thoughts were interrupted by Joe shouting at her from the back room. "The Linotype's acting up again. Call Rob and get him to pick up that part we've been needing when he makes his run to Wilmington."

Laurel placed the call and swung her attention back to her work. The day had started in earnest now. An hour later Joan called. "Mayor Boggs wants to talk to you, Laurel," she explained. "Could you come over here to the office sometime soon?"

"Right away," Laurel agreed. Picking up her keys and purse, she explained to Joe where she was going and set off down the main street to the long, low building that housed the police station and the mayor's office.

Everyone she passed spoke to her, and at least two of the older ladies in town openly admired her new outfit.

Heavens, she thought with wry humor, had she been looking that bad?

Joan took one look at her and arched her eyebrows in surprise. "Any special reason why you're all dressed up?" she asked. "Don't tell me you did it for the mayor?" Both of them laughed at that. The mayor was a fat, balding, stocky little man, full of self-importance—a very unlikely target for romance.

"Just thought I needed some new clothes," Laurel said defensively. "Nothing special."

Joan eyed her consideringly for a moment and then shrugged. "Well, whatever your reason, I approve of the change."

The door to the inner office opened and the mayor came out, smiling and wiping his broad forehead with a large handkerchief. "Why, hello, Laurel, didn't think you'd get here so soon." He shook her hand with a slightly moist palm and led the way into his office.

"We're thinking about selling the land," he told her bluntly once they were seated. "Now, now," he said crossly when she started to speak. "I know you don't approve. But the town needs money, money for some additions to the high school, and money for several of our social programs."

"What about holding out for government funds?" Laurel finally interjected. "If we wait, they might consider assuming responsibility for the land as part of the National Seashore."

"It would be too late, Laurel. You know how sticky bureaucratic red tape gets and how long it takes to untangle it. We need that money in our coffers soon, and an opportunity like this may not come up again. Besides, Lockner's offering us a good price, a good price indeed.

The government would never match it. I've recommended to the council that they approve the sale."

"There *must* be some other way to raise the money," Laurel protested with growing desperation.

"There isn't," the mayor said flatly. "We can't raise the taxes any higher; people won't stand for it. This is the only way."

"Don't you realize what Lockner is going to do with that land?" Laurel's voice rose slightly. "His builders will move in and throw up some unsightly structure, using advertising and hard-sell tactics to bring in people from all over. The beach will be closed off, and the townspeople won't be able to use it any more."

"I know, I know." He wiped his forehead nervously. "It's not much of a choice—beaches or schools? But which is more important? Think about it, Laurel."

"Joan says you've called a town meeting for Thursday," Laurel said tightly, ignoring his last observation.

"We want to give everyone in town a chance to voice his or her opinion," the mayor acknowledged. "You can be sure what the people will decide, though. Lockner will get that land."

He came around the side of the desk and awkwardly patted her shoulder. "I am sorry, Laurel, but there's nothing I can do."

Out in the lobby again, Laurel stopped and waited until Joan hung up the telephone. "Got time for a quick break?" she asked.

Joan glanced indecisively at the door of the mayor's office and then agreed. "Might as well. Shall we go over to the coffee shop?"

A few minutes later they were seated in the town's only luncheonette, Joan drinking a cup of tea and Laurel sipping on a cola. "What did he tell you?" Joan asked curiously.

"What you'd already told me," Laurel shrugged. "He's recommended that they sell."

"It looks pretty definite," Joan agreed. "From what I saw of Mr. Lockner, he'll be able to talk the council into doing whatever he wants them to do."

"You met him?" Laurel queried.

"Yesterday." Joan stirred her tea absently. "I told you when we met for lunch, remember? He came into the office right before I called you."

"Young?" asked Laurel.

"Early thirties I'd say." Joan rolled her eyes expressively. "Quite a man. I didn't get to talk to him, though. He only stayed with the mayor a few minutes and then dashed out in a hurry."

"Probably doesn't want to waste any more time than he has to on small-town people like us," Laurel observed bitterly.

"He didn't seem like that at all," protested Joan. "I got the impression he was simply in a hurry."

"Had to rush out and make another million, I suppose." Laurel finished her drink and put some money on the counter with the check. Swinging around on the stool, she stared out through the window.

"I wonder if he's really as wealthy as they say he is," Joan said idly, still sipping her tea.

"Who, Lockner?" Laurel asked, regrouping her wandering thoughts.

"From what they say about him, he's a shrewd businessman."

Joan's voice vaguely irritated Laurel. She really seemed to have taken a liking to this Lockner man.

"Wonder if he's married?" Joan continued. "Hey, that's an idea. Maybe you could get him to fall for you. That way you could keep your lighthouse and get him, too!" Joan's dark eyes were flashing with amusement. "Now that I think of it, he might be just your type."

"Don't be ridiculous," Laurel snapped shortly. "He's the last man on earth I'd have anything to do with."

Joan looked at her steadily and prodded, "When are you going to forget Vince?" Her voice was quiet but relentless. "You're making a mistake if you judge all men by him."

Laurel refused to answer her, changing the subject abruptly. Vince wasn't the man on her mind right now, but she didn't want Joan to know that.

By the time she returned to the newspaper office, her mind had blocked out the conversation with Joan. She had two more days ahead of her before the town meeting, two days in which to convince enough of the townspeople to resist the movement to sell the lighthouse to Lockner.

That afternoon Laurel began calling people, talking to friends of her father and people she'd known all her life, begging them to support her in her fight to retain the lighthouse. Everyone agreed with her, it seemed. That is, they understood her desire to preserve the old building. But all of them talked of the town's need for money, reluctantly stressing that the necessities of the present had to supersede the relics of the past. And they all displayed a remarkable lack of faith in the possibility that their stretch of beach would ever become part of the National Seashore.

By Wednesday evening, Laurel had to admit she was discouraged. Her chances of winning the fight against the Lockner Development Corporation were looking slimmer and slimmer. She bitterly pondered the fact that people never appreciated what they had until they lost it.

She stretched her slender legs out in front of her and rubbed a weary hand across the stiff muscles of her neck, sore from bending over her desk all day.

Joe had left hours ago, fussing at her as he left because she wasn't going upstairs to her own apartment. "Haven't you got a date with Howard tonight?" he'd demanded. "When I was your age I went out every night."

"Why don't you go on home, Joe," Laurel had laughed affectionately. Now she had to ask herself that question.

Climbing the stairs, she decided to take a long bath. Maybe that would soothe her tired muscles and help her sleep. She ran the tub full of steamy water, pouring in a handful of bath beads and slipped out of her clothes.

Stretching out in the warm water, she leaned back, closing her eyes, her mind drifting helplessly to thoughts of Drew. It seemed running away hadn't solved her problem. Why hadn't she realized that once Drew possessed her body completely, she would belong to him, be incomplete and lonely without him?

Ever since Monday she had looked up whenever someone walked past the windows of the newspaper office, searching for Drew's lean, muscular figure and thick brown hair. Every time the phone rang her hands shook slightly as she picked up the receiver, wondering if this time she would hear his low, warm voice saying, "Laurel?"

Why had she refused to find out more about him? Was it her way of not admitting to herself that she wanted him? A defense against the truth of how important he could become to her?

She couldn't go on like this much longer. After tomorrow night she would look for him. It shouldn't be hard to locate an artist living in the Wilmington area.

Thursday morning dawned sunny and mild, and Laurel woke up with a sense of purpose. Tonight would decide the fate of her beloved lighthouse. Even though it didn't look hopeful, she was determined to fight until the last possible moment.

The day couldn't pass quickly enough for her. Several times she caught herself glancing at the clock, willing it to hurry up so she would be able to get this evening over and done with.

For once she closed the office promptly at five so she'd have enough time to eat dinner and dress carefully for the meeting. For some reason she felt she had to look her best, if only because she was afraid the news was going to be bad.

Most of her dinner was left untasted, her stomach too knotted to tolerate food. She bathed leisurely, trying to relax her taut muscles and ward off the headache that was beginning to pound at her temples.

Drying off with a thick, fluffy towel, she slid into delicate, gossamer-thin panties and bra, pulled on a pair of sheer pantyhose, and then slipped into the coral knit dress. It clung softly to her slim figure, giving her a graceful, calm look that was a study in contrast to her churning emotions.

Brushing her hair until it shone, she arranged it in soft waves around her face, applying a little mascara to emphasize the thick curve of her eyelashes and highlighting her cheeks with a shimmering blush.

The Laurel who looked back at her was infinitely different from the one she'd seen in this very mirror less than a week ago. Her polished appearance gave her an air of confidence she was far from feeling, providing a protective shield for the battle ahead of her.

Snatching up her purse, she hurried down to her car, leaving a lone light burning above the doorway.

The drive to the high school building took only a few minutes. Town meetings were always held in the school auditorium; it was the only room large enough to hold all the residents in the surrounding area.

Joan was there ahead of her, seated on the platform in front of the auditorium, the mayor's plump wife beside her. "Another new outfit?" Joan smiled at Laurel in surprise.

Briefly shrugging her shoulders, Laurel asked, "Where am I supposed to sit?"

"Right over there." Joan gestured to the far side of the platform. "Mayor Boggs will be on your right side and they've put Mr. Lockner on your left."

"Is he here already?" Laurel looked around the room hastily, seeing only the familiar faces of townspeople.

"Not yet, but he should be here any minute." Joan turned back to Mrs. Boggs.

Laurel wandered around the room for a while, stopping to speak to old friends, taking this last opportunity to coax them to join her defense of the lighthouse.

"I enjoyed your editorial today," several people told her, holding up copies of *The Beacon* and pointing to the black-and-white photo of the lighthouse on the front page. No one, however, assured her he or she would vote against the sale.

As Mrs. Grimes, the high school music teacher, moved over to the piano to play the usual opening songs, Laurel hurried back to the platform. The meeting was beginning.

The mayor was already seated, the two chairs beside him still empty. Laurel sat down next to him, gesturing to the empty seat on her left side. "Where's Mr. Lockner?" she whispered.

"Late," the mayor hissed. "He'll be here soon."

Mrs. Grimes completed her piano overture, and the head of the town council gave the welcoming speech. Town meetings always followed the same pattern, never altering their course, even when a controversial issue was at stake. Why, oh why, Laurel wondered, couldn't the strong sense of tradition tacitly implied in this procedure carry over into more important matters, like preserving the lighthouse from the encroachment of so-called progress?

The chair beside her remained stubbornly empty, the elusive Mr. Lockner still mysteriously absent. Maybe he's changed his mind, she thought hopefully. Maybe he doesn't want the land after all. So involved was she in her eleventh-hour wishes she scarcely noticed as the mayor got up beside her and moved to the microphone. He was characteristically long-winded, spending a great deal of time on the routine matter of outlining the issues to be discussed. Laurel barely listened, her attention focused on what she herself planned to say. She abruptly came to her senses as a small stir swept through the audience.

The mayor was looking toward the back of the auditorium, his words booming out over the audience. "...and now Mr. Lockner will speak to you about the offer he is making for our land."

Laurel followed his gaze to the man who was striding down the side aisle of the auditorium. Her eyes blinked several times and then widened, a ripple of shock registering in her stunned consciousness. It was impossible! There had to be some mistake. Her mind was having difficulty perceiving the messages it was receiving from her confused senses. The familiar dark brown hair, the strong, broad shoulders. *No*, her heart screamed.

It was true. By some incredible, unbelievable, horrible mistake it was true. Mr. J. A. Lockner and her mysterious weekend companion were one and the same man.

She sat immobile as he reached the platform, his gaze sliding over her frozen figure. He nodded briefly, secret recognition lighting his glittering brown eyes.

As he turned and stopped in front of the lectern, her brain slowly registered his altered appearance. Gone were the faded jeans, the flannel shirts. The figure standing before the audience tonight was clad in a flawless gray suit with an elegant white shirt, the French cuffs of which bore heavy gold cufflinks. From the impeccably creased trousers to the broad knot in his silk tie, his clothes bore the unmistakable marks of fine tailoring. He faced the audience confidently, his friendly, relaxed manner winning them instantly to his side.

Even though she knew without a doubt that this was Drew, her confused mind refused to believe it. How could she have been so misled by him? It just couldn't be true. Drew couldn't possibly be this successful businessman, this tycoon! Even as she watched, he pulled out a pair of glasses, undoubtedly designer frames, and put them on, pulling a sheaf of notes out of his pocket and beginning to speak.

She barely saw the mayor come back and sit down beside her; she missed the first words Drew said to the audience. Trying desperately to put the facts together, she could come up with one reality: Drew had tricked her.

Her numbed mind began to thaw, a raging anger sweeping through her icy veins. How dare he! He'd known all along who *she* was. He'd known how she felt about him. Everyone involved in this sale knew that Laurel Grey, editor of *The Beacon*, was the major opponent of the Lockner Development Corporation. And he had deliberately withheld his identity from her. He had deliberately—

Here her mental process stopped. She couldn't believe that. She wouldn't have set out to seduce her in order to persuade her to change her mind about the land. Or would he? After all, what did she know about him? The warm ideas she'd been nurturing about Drew had just been knocked into a heap, made a sham, an illusion, by the reality that he was James Lockner. He'd even lied about his first name. There wasn't even a remote connection between the two names, James and Drew—by no stretch of the imagination could Drew be a nickname for James.

He must have been laughing at her all weekend, she fumed inwardly. "Know your enemy," he'd told her laughingly. She shuddered when she realized just how intimately she'd gotten to know him.

Laurel squared her shoulders and lifted her chin. He'd had his last laugh at her expense. She knew her enemy now, all right!

Although struggling frantically inside, she rallied her customary poise, calming herself deliberately, forcing herself to concentrate on what Drew was saying. What *James* was saying, she reminded herself coldly.

"There are those here tonight who would freeze time,

stop all progress, impede the future growth of this area," he was saying. "I have nothing against preserving the past. I daresay my roots go as deep as those of anyone present tonight. But there is a greater consideration before us, and that is the economic one. Besides solving some of the immediate problems of the town's schools, I will be adding jobs and trade to the local community."

Laurel was screaming inwardly. How dare he? He was practically quoting the facts she had supplied that day at the lighthouse. She'd told him herself that the town needed money for the schools! Oh, his arguments were persuasive all right—and she'd fed him all his best lines.

Her mind was running smoothly by the time he finished speaking, her thoughts cold and deliberate, focused totally on the issues at hand.

For a moment her poise threatened to desert her as Drew crossed the platform and sat down in the chair beside her. In spite of reason, in spite of what she'd just learned, her senses cried out at his nearness, her mind flashing back to that night on the beach.

By a sheer act of will she managed to leave her seat as the mayor introduced her, walking to the lectern with calm, unhurried steps, placing her notes on its surface carefully before beginning to speak.

Repressed anger made her arguments cool and logical. Her mouth formed the words she'd rehearsed that very afternoon even while her mind kept jumping back to thoughts of Drew. Slowly her voice gathered strength as she watched the friendly, sympathetic faces before her.

As she neared the end of her speech, she ad-libbed, "Frankly, I distrust those who speak out of both sides of their mouths. They're all too willing to avow a love for the past—until their own plans, their own ambitions, are in danger of being thwarted. Unless we make a united stand against such ruthless destruction of what we cherish, soon we will have nothing left by which to remember our unique North Carolina heritage."

When her speech was completed there was a wide round of applause before the mayor rose again to take the microphone. Laurel managed to get back to her seat without looking directly at Drew, not trusting herself to meet his gaze. Once seated, their knees nearly touched, his neatly trousered leg unnervingly close to her own soft skirt. She twisted away with a quick movement and was instantly sorry. After all, they were on view for everyone to see!

She listened tautly while a vote was taken. The town council would make the final decision of course, but they would seriously consider the opinion voiced here tonight. It seemed to take an inordinate amount of time. The mayor's ponderous voice, the slow tabulation by the several assistants who were stationed at various points around the auditorium, went on interminably.

Her heart sank as the results were announced. By a large margin the townspeople recommended that the sale to Lockner be put through. It was virtually decided then; there was almost no hope her land could be saved.

With a start she realized that Mayor Boggs was calling the meeting to a close. Instantly she felt trapped. Her exit was effectively blocked by Drew's chair. There was no possible way she could get past him without speaking.

The very moment the meeting was over, Laurel jumped to her feet. She was too late. Drew had also risen, his lean figure so near she could feel the warmth emanating from his body. Inevitably her gaze lifted to his, and their glances locked for endless moments. His face was painfully familiar, serious now, the smile gone from his dark eyes.

He reached out and grasped her arm lightly, his fingers burning her soft skin. "Laurel," he said, his voice low and hurried.

"Don't waste your charm on me, Mr. Lockner," Laurel hissed. She was acutely conscious of the people around her, and she kept her voice low.

"You at least acknowledge I have charm?" He had a dry note in his voice, and the copper eyes flicked over her questioningly.

Across the room she saw Joe threading through the crowd toward them, camera in hand. She smiled. "I'm sure you keep in practice."

"Thank you. I appreciate your endorsement."

Laurel blinked at the flash of the camera, keeping a bland expression on her face. "I hope you don't mind getting front-page coverage in such a countrified newspaper," she said between clenched teeth.

"Not as long as editorial opinion is confined to its proper place." His soft voice infuriated her. Was he actually so cold-hearted that he was enjoying making her squirm like this?

Mayor Boggs came up behind them and clasped a hand on Drew's shoulder. "Marvelous. Both of you. Don't know when I've heard a more spirited debate," his voice boomed out.

"Thank you." Laurel turned her back on Drew and waved at Joan, who was making her way toward the doorway. "Someone is waiting for me." She smiled vaguely. "Please excuse me, Mayor."

Joan was standing near the entrance to the auditorium.

"I'm sorry about the way things turned out," she said softly, her eyes anxious.

"It's not final yet," Laurel said quietly. "Not until the council actually votes." She smiled shakily and said, "I'll talk to you tomorrow. Right now, I'm going home. I've got a slight headache." With that hurriedly mumbled excuse she walked quickly to her car.

A gleaming red Chrysler LeBaron convertible was parked near her car, its sleek lines and luxurious upholstery looking oddly out of place among the older cars that flanked it. It was undoubtedly *his* car, she realized.

Her own auto made a sad contrast with the luxury model he drove—as sad a contrast as their owners made. The Drew she'd known at the lighthouse was an illusion. The reality was behind her in the school building, a remote, ruthless businessman who would go to any lengths to get what he wanted. She would have to keep reminding herself of that fact—or risk splintering into a million jagged fragments.

CHAPTER NINE

THE DRIVE BACK to her apartment took only a few minutes. It was a bright, moonlit night, the dark sky twinkling with a myriad of stars, but Laurel's attention was far away as she drove through the sleepy streets. She parked her car behind her building and went upstairs slowly, her steps lagging as she reached the top. Without turning on any lights she sat down in front of the window, gazing out at the darkened street, her thoughts confused, her mind tired.

She thought of the way she had surrendered to him. He had been relentless in his seduction, fooling her with sensual gentleness but ultimately forcing her to succumb.

What had happened to the independent woman she had once been? The woman who was in control of her own life, charting her own destiny. Had it all been an illusion, a carefully constructed facade that had crumbled under his fiery assault on her senses?

Conflicting feelings threatened to overwhelm her.

Loathing for her own weakness in responding to his seductive caresses mingled with anger at the way he had pried into her life, stripping away her privacy, laying bare the wild longing inside her that only he could satisfy.

At last she pulled the drapes across the window and went into the bedroom, taking off the knit dress. Slipping into the coral nightgown, she lay down on the bed, staring up at the ceiling, her muscles taut and tense.

The faint sound of an engine idling beneath her window made her sit up, her body stiffening with an unwelcome sense of expectancy. She knew instinctively who it was. The engine stopped and a car door slammed, firm steps treading the distance to the front door of the office.

A loud knock resounded through the room below, and Laurel froze. Thank goodness she hadn't turned on any lights. Maybe he would go away, decide she wasn't home. Even as she thought that, the doorknob rattled insistently, the knocking beginning again.

She stood up, moving over quietly to stand by the bedroom door, staring indecisively down the stairs.

"Laurel," he called out, his voice echoing in the empty street. She threw on a thin white cotton robe and hurried down the steps, her feet bare, her hair flowing over her shoulders.

"Go away," she hissed loudly through the glass, glaring furiously at the silhouette of his body outside the shaded window.

"Let me in," he urged. "I want to talk to you."

"I have nothing to say to you," she called out. "Go away."

His voice suddenly boomed emphatically in the quiet

street. "I want to talk to you about the weekend we spent together."

Laurel opened the door in a burst of speed, her eyes flashing with dark fury. "Do you want everyone in town to hear you?" she demanded in an angry whisper.

He had one foot over the doorstep before she realized what he was doing. As the rest of his body followed into the office, he grinned at her with satisfaction. "I knew that would work."

"Get out," she ordered fiercely. "Just get out of here now."

Drew turned away from her calmly, walking around the dark, cluttered little office, his steps reverberating in the silence.

He calmly turned on a light, examined a faded picture of her great-grandfather holding the first edition of *The Beacon*, then sauntered over to look at a row of trophies on a wooden shelf. "So this is where you work," he said finally. "It's exactly how I pictured it."

Her spine rigid with anger, Laurel waited by the door without speaking.

"You might as well close the door," he told her quietly. "And why don't you invite me upstairs and offer me something to drink? You weren't so inhospitable last weekend."

Laurel found her voice at last, slamming the door behind her with a furious snap. "How dare you mention last weekend, you swine, you liar, you—"

"Scoundrel?" he supplied laughingly. "Or perhaps you'd prefer something a little more forceful." He paused for a moment, walking toward her slowly. "I'm the one who should be angry, Laurel," he said, his voice sounding dangerously quiet and calm. "After all, you're the one who left without so much as a good-bye. You ran out, leaving me without saying a word, without even asking how I planned to get back to town."

"It looks like you made it just fine," Laurel flared, her voice vibrating with hostility.

Drew moved over to stand directly in front of her, his dark gaze burning down into her uplifted face. "Why did you run?" he asked, his voice deadly calm. "Just tell me why you ran."

"I don't think I owe you any explanations," Laurel said from between clenched teeth. Taking a step backwards, she groped for the railing on the stairway. "And what shall I call you, Mr. Lockner? Is it James, or Drew— or do you change the name to fit the occasion?"

"My name is Drew," he said calmly. "I told you the truth. For the record, my middle name is Andrew. Since my father was a James, my parents called me Drew to avoid confusion."

"You knew I'd never guess who you were," she accused angrily. "Why didn't you tell me the whole truth?"

"Perhaps I was afraid you'd leave me out on the doorstep." His voice was amused, his shoulders lifting in a slight shurg. "After all, it was raining, and I was left to your tender mercies."

"You knew who I was all along," she said, her voice painfully taut.

"I knew before you mentioned the newspaper," he agreed quietly, his voice devoid of any sort of apology.

Outside the window, a car came down the street slowly, its headlights beaming through the plate glass and forcing Laurel to take a hasty step back into the shadows. "If we stand here talking, someone will see us," she ground out. "In a small town, it doesn't do for the editor of the newspaper to be seen entertaining male visitors at this hour of the night."

"Always proper, that's you," he said lightly. "Then shall we go upstairs?"

"No! Why don't you just leave," Laurel ordered, blocking the stairway with her slim figure.

"We haven't finished our conversation." His voice held a note of finality that defied argument. With a surge of fury she led the way upstairs. In this mood there was no telling how much of a scene he was capable of creating.

Her small living room was dark, the thick drapes across the window blocking out any trace of light from the street. Laurel led the way across to the old, upholstered chairs before the window and switched on a low lamp. As Drew's gaze swept over the length of her figure, she became aware of the sheer fabric of her gown, the gauzy cotton robe.

Pulling the lapels of the robe closely about her neck, she gestured to a chair without speaking. Instead of sitting down, Drew walked slowly about the room, looking at the cluster of family photographs on a small table in the corner, spending long moments scanning the few paintings on the walls. His studied deliberation grated on her nerves, making her want to scream out accusations at him, arouse and inflame him in the same way he did her.

Finally he turned back to her, his expression unreadable. "You've always lived here?" he asked in the tone of a person making a social call.

Laurel was steaming. He didn't seem to be aware of

her unwelcoming attitude. Did he really believe she would want to talk to him? Didn't he realize she was through with him?

When she didn't answer he walked slowly around the room again before sitting down on her small sofa. He'd removed his reading glasses, but he still looked like a stranger, his expensive suit and finely tailored shirt making her own possessions look shabby by contrast.

"What do you want?" she asked, barely recognizing the sound of her own voice, its tones low and husky and filled with only slightly repressed fury.

"I want to know why you left on Sunday without saying a word." This time his voice held a trace of anger too, demanding an explanation and brooking no opposition.

"That's none of your business," Laurel flared.

"On the contrary." His voice was low, almost menacing in its quality. "I think it's very much my business. After what happened"—his voice became more forceful—"I didn't expect to wake up and find you gone."

Barely maintaining a facade of cool dignity, Laurel shrugged her shoulders with an effort, laughing slightly. "What did you expect? Declarations of undying love?" She forced a note of amusement into her voice. "I hardly think that would have fit the occasion."

His eyes narrowed, his face shutting down into an unreadable mask. Before he could speak Laurel found herself again asking the question she wasn't sure she wanted an answer to. "Why did you keep your identity a secret?" Her voice shook slightly. "You made sure you told me nothing about yourself."

He looked up at her, holding her gaze with a seriousness that made her flush nervously. "You never asked anything about me, Laurel," he responded simply. "As I remember, you were very careful to avoid making a single question about my life. You never even asked my last name."

Laurel wanted to deny what he was saying, but her basic honesty refused to allow her to lie to herself. He was right; she hadn't asked any questions. She hadn't intended to get involved with this man.

She had been afraid, scared of the intensity of her own response to him. Afraid the tenuous relationship he offered, based solely on sexual attraction, would reopen old wounds, scar her, leave her robbed of all she'd struggled to achieve.

It was ironic; she'd been right. There was a huge gulf between the man who sat on the other side of the room and herself. Not only were they adversaries in the fight for the lighthouse—there was much more to it than that— but also everything about his life-style was abhorrent to her. His obvious wealth, his high-powered business tactics, his casual use of deception—all of this made it perfectly clear he would only destroy her if she let him get close to her again.

"You don't like the truth, Laurel," he accused softly. "You already had your ideas about the head of the Lockner Development Corporation definitively formed. Without any real facts, without knowing anything about me, you condemned me as a ruthless, money-grubbing, unfeeling bastard. Now you're angry because you don't want to admit you could actually find something likable about the man you were supposed to hate. You can't accept the fact that you let a man like that make love to you."

"That's not true," Laurel retorted. "I never hated you

personally. How could I? I don't hate people I've never met. But I didn't like your business tactics, and I still don't. I don't like the way you've bought up land along the coast and thrown up a lot of quick, money-making buildings." She didn't add her aversion to the power he held over her, the way his expert lovemaking reduced her to a helpless, mindless state.

"What exactly do you know about my business tactics?" Drew asked, his voice dangerously calm and quiet. "Where have you gotten your information? I don't recall that you ever came to me and asked me personally about my business."

Laurel was silent for a moment. It was irritating to have to admit that there was an element of truth in what he said. Her father had always insisted that every word the newspaper printed be backed up with solid evidence. Lately she'd been so busy it had become increasingly difficult for her to thoroughly research every article.

"Perhaps you're right," she conceded. "But that doesn't change the fact that you're wrong about the lighthouse. You're in such a hurry to make money, to see your company grow, that you've forgotten this area has a past. You've let your goals for the future overshadow the rich history of the area, the human element."

With a sudden change of direction Drew's voice became silky, seductive. "On the contrary, Laurel, I'm very interested in the human element." As his gaze slid suggestively down the length of her, Laurel realized the old robe was doing very little to conceal the curves of her figure beneath the sheer gown. She flinched as Drew stood up lithely, quickly shortening the distance between them.

Helplessly she watched as he moved closer, standing

absolutely still as he wound a strand of her hair around his finger and placed his other hand at the curve of her waist. She was unable to protest as he pulled her against him, her mouth dry, her heart racing with a strange mixture of apprehension and expectancy.

She stared into his observant eyes, hypnotized by his intense scrutiny. A denial rose to her lips even as their mouths met, his lips forcing hers apart, exploring with a breathless warmth that kindled fires in every nerve ending.

Why was she always weak like this when Drew touched her? Where was the self-control she valued so much? She tried pulling away, but his arms were like bands of steel around her slender waist, his mouth possessive and subjugating.

As she curled against his hard, masculine length she felt the past few hours slipping away, forgetting the moment when she had found out her weekend companion was James Lockner, forgetting that they were enemies. Instead, she surrendered to the remembered feel of his arms and lips, the rising surge of desire, the familiar touch of the Drew she had known during those few hours on the beach.

With fingers that trembled slightly she pushed the suit jacket from his shoulders even as he tugged her more firmly against him. She had stopped fighting her own feelings for the moment. It was so much easier to simply give in to her desire, to pretend for even a short time that they were back at the lighthouse, the tide running strongly, the pounding of her pulse matching the rhythm of the surf.

Drew swept her into his arms and carried her back to the sofa, settling himself down on its worn surface and pulling her against his body. Her robe had slipped off her shoulders and she heard him laugh slightly as he commented, "Quite an improvement over the pajamas." Then his lips were on hers again, his tongue probing insistently, demanding full access to the soft recesses of her mouth. She moaned softly, whispering his name in hoarse breaths, reveling in the familiar feel of his body, the sensations his touch never failed to arouse.

After pushing the robe to the floor, he slid the flimsy straps of her nightgown down her arms, nudging the silky material all the way to her waist. A husky murmur of pleasure rose from his throat as he felt her shivery response. Laurel arched her body against his touch, a fire burning through her veins as he caressed the soft flesh of her breasts, his thumbs brushing her taut nipples.

She watched as he pulled away slightly to one-handedly tug off his tie and unbutton his shirt, revealing the wide, muscled shoulders and bronzed chest. She strained forward, seeking the heat and hardness of his body, a muffled moan of excitement escaping her lips as his mouth once more moved down over her flesh, teasing and tormenting with sensual kisses.

He lowered her on the cushions until she was lying on her back, her breasts exposed to his hungry gaze, his body partially covering her smooth legs beneath the filmy barrier of her nightgown. His mouth returned to hers, exploring, demanding a response her body was eager to give. His hands gently kneaded her breasts, his lips and tongue traced a fiery path across their rosy tips. Laurel had no strength to resist, giving him the quivering response he seemed to crave, reveling in his low murmurs of pleasure and passion.

"Please, Drew," she cried softly, pushing his shirt off

his shoulders, pulling him more closely against her, pressing her fingers into the ridges of his shoulders.

"Please what?" he whispered. He wrapped her into his arms, his hands sliding the nightgown completely off her slender legs, roaming everywhere on the soft curves of her naked body, discovering all her secret, responsive places.

Her drugged mind was slowly succumbing to the desire raging through her, dreaming only of the consuming need to be possessed by him again, to be caught up in the exquisite pleasure only he could give her.

She had forgotten her distrust of him, her anger, her fear of being controlled. Everything but her need for him had been drained from her, and she moaned with pleasure, digging her fingers into his back, writhing beneath him.

The phone rang shrilly. Drew pulled back, swearing softly under his breath. "Don't answer it," he whispered.

She tried to disregard the sharp, insistent ringing. Every nerve in her body throbbed with an aching desire for fulfillment. As the phone continued to ring—ten, eleven times—she lay frozen, indecisive, her mind refusing to ignore the persistent clamor.

Drew finally sighed and sat up, his breathing ragged as he sought to regain control. With an impatient gesture he reached for the receiver.

The autocratic action suddenly infuriated Laurel, and she slid past him, jerking the phone from its stand, glaring at him with widened eyes. Her voice trembled slightly as she answered.

"I couldn't wait to hear if you won the lighthouse fight." Howard's good-natured voice floated over the line.

Laurel flinched, shifting uneasily until she was able to grasp her nightgown and hold it around her shivering body, carefully avoiding Drew's eyes as she said, "It's nice of you to call, Howard, but I'm afraid it's hopeless." She carefully steadied her voice as she added, "It's difficult to fight someone who'll go to any lengths to get what he wants."

Drew reached out and grasped Laurel's chin, tilting her face around until she was forced to look at him. "Hang up," he hissed.

Laurel refused to respond, listening as Howard sympathized effusively, enjoying the leaping rage in Drew's eyes as she said, "I'd love to see your new car. I should have some time tomorrow afternoon if you'd like to take me for a ride."

Drew pulled on his shirt and buttoned it with deliberate, controlled movements before picking up his tie and jacket. Laurel took bitter pleasure from the furious glances he cast her way, prolonging her conversation with Howard far beyond their usual limits. His call had come at the right moment, keeping her from giving in to thoughtless desire, reminding her of Drew's treachery.

Howard at last said good-bye, and Laurel was forced to put down the phone. Drew's lean body was tense, anger evident in every movement he made, as he grasped her arm, pulling her down until she sat beside him on the couch.

"Why did you do that?" he demanded. "You want me; you can't hide that."

"No, I don't," she denied with a deliberate calm.

"Don't lie to me," he said roughly. "We both know what we wanted tonight. In another few minutes—"

"Stop it," she said angrily, reaching for the thin cotton

robe on the floor, wrapping it around herself and clutching its meager folds against her body.

"What kind of game are you playing, Laurel?" His anger was white hot now, fine lines etched around his compressed lips. "I'm afraid I don't know the rules to this one."

"I'm not playing games. I made a mistake last weekend. I don't want to repeat it."

He muttered an oath savagely, striding across to the doorway of her tiny kitchen and stopping with his back turned toward her.

"I'm not looking for an affair," Laurel told him, her voice sounding unnaturally loud in the quiet room.

"I don't recall asking you to have one," he said forcefully. "You're jumping to conclusions again. Not looking at all the facts."

What facts? she cried silently. The ones you want me to believe, or what I know to be true? Her lips were unable to form the question, unable to direct the words at his unyielding back. When he didn't say anything more, she pronounced, "It's very late. You'd better leave."

Drew turned around and walked slowly back toward her, his face closed and shuttered. "I'm leaving," he enunciated carefully. "I don't think we can say anything else to each other tonight."

When she didn't speak he said, "You're coming to my home for dinner tomorrow night."

"I am not," Laurel said flatly.

"Oh yes you are." The anger in his voice was quiet, the control in his tones making his stance seem somehow threatening. "I've invited the mayor and the town council to my place so we can discuss the final aspects of the sale."

"It's not final yet," she flared.

"It will be," he said, the confidence in his voice making the hairs prickle on the back of her neck.

"Don't be so sure of yourself," she spat furiously. "And I won't be there, thank you."

"Yes you will," he reaffirmed, leaning so close she inched back. "You'll be there because you'll do almost anything to keep your lighthouse." With that he strode off down the steps. The echoing sound of the slamming door seemed to linger long after his car had driven away.

CHAPTER TEN

LAUREL TURNED ON the television with a defiant gesture when Drew left, attempting to block out her thoughts; but the light chatter on the late evening talk show only made her nerves vibrate more.

Wearily she crawled into bed, the flush of victory she had felt over angering Drew quickly fading away. Why deny that if Howard hadn't called there would have been no stopping her response to his seduction?

One moment she had been furious, mentally denouncing the way he'd kept the truth of his identity from her. Then, before she was even aware of the change, desire had run through her so fast she'd forgotten everything except the flare of passion as the last shreds of her resistance melted away under his warm, persuasive caresses.

Her face burned with humiliation. If determination wasn't the solution to her problem, what was? This time the pain was too deep for tears, and she lay sleepless for hours, her eyes wide but unseeing, her throat dry and aching with suppressed emotion.

One look in the mirror the next morning convinced Laurel of the need to hide her ravaged emotions under a layer of makeup. Her eyes were shadowed and dark, faint circles giving evidence of her lack of sleep. She slipped into jeans and a cotton shirt, rolling up the sleeves and leaving the collar open at her throat.

At least today was Friday. For her and Joe this was usually the only relaxed weekday. The paper was already out, the first flurry of comments and complaints already dispatched. Joe usually took Friday morning off. With the next edition still days off, nothing seemed too pressing.

Laurel walked down the steps slowly, glancing around the familiar room, wondering what it had looked like to Drew. His eyes had revealed nothing as they'd searched the corners and studied the battered file cabinets, the ancient typewriter, the overflowing bookcases lining the walls. She shrugged impatiently. What difference did his opinion make anyway?

Today the office seemed empty and chilly. A pile of letters lay on the floor in front of the mail slot. Laurel picked them up, fingering them idly.

Probably replies to her editorial. Local people took the issues seriously and frequently fired off letters to let the editor know their own opinions. She slit open several envelopes, scanning the contents indifferently. It was the same old story. While they appreciated her efforts to save the beach and lighthouse, they felt her plans were impractical without substantial financial backing.

One or two letters expressed unconditional support,

and Laurel felt a quick pang of sadness. Their help was appreciated, but it was probably too late.

The phone rang, and Laurel took a deep breath before answering its imperious ring. Her day had begun. She had no time to mope. The secretary of the school board called requesting help with a report she was writing. The new owner of the hardware store wanted a quote on advertising rates, and several people called to tell her their classified ads had brought quick results.

By the time the sheriff stopped by to express his appreciation for her help on this year's benefit dance committee, the morning had flown by. There was no way Laurel could face a lonely lunch upstairs.

She dialed Joan's number quickly. "How about running by Kelly's and picking up a couple of those delicious crab burgers? I'll make some coffee, and we can eat here in the office."

"They're fattening," Joan moaned, "but I'll be there."

The girls munched companionably on their sandwiches, Joan studiously avoiding any mention of the meeting the evening before. Laurel hated the knowledge that her friend was pitying her, but at least Joan had no idea how deep the hurt really lay.

Laurel was gathering up the remnants of their lunch when the front door swung open. Papers scattered from the desk, some falling to the floor.

Joan smoothed down her skirt, nervously clearing her throat. For several moments Laurel eyed the man in the doorway defensively. Who did he think he was to barge in here like this, upsetting her routine, embarrassing her in front of Joan?

Under his relentless gaze she found her voice, saying firmly, "The office is usually closed during lunch, Mr.

Lockner. Since you're from out of town, I'll make an exception this time."

An amused smile lit his brown eyes. "That's kind of you, Laurel," he said smoothly, emphasizing his use of her first name, "but this is more on the order of a social call." Smiling broadly at Joan, he pulled up a chair and sat down beside her.

Laurel sat in the worn leather chair behind her desk, alert and poised. The hairs on the back of her neck rose in response to his presence, warning her not to let down her guard for a moment.

Joan broke the silence, reaching over to the table and pouring a cup of coffee. "I believe you like your coffee black," she said sweetly.

"Your memory's excellent," he acknowledged, taking a sip and eyeing Laurel with lurking humor. After draining his cup he said, "Beautiful day, isn't it? Perfect for a picnic on the beach, I'd say."

"Perfect," Laurel agreed evenly, ignoring the implication in his eyes and words. "Though I imagine a busy man like you wouldn't have much leisure time."

"That's where you're wrong. I'm not a workaholic like you."

"Aren't you making a snap judgment?" she flared.

"You'd never catch me having lunch in my office," he pointed out, including Joan in his smile.

Joan flushed and said quickly, "That's what I tell Laurel all the time. She needs to relax more and enjoy life."

"Who says I'm not enjoying life?" returned Laurel, irritated by the blatant charm in Drew's manner; it was all for Joan's benefit, of course.

"Laurel does know how to have fun," Joan began defending in a friendly voice.

"I'm sure she does," he agreed, his eyes sending a secret message, which Laurel ignored.

"She's only unfriendly now because of how much she loves her lighthouse," Joan offered helpfully.

"Heavens," Laurel interrupted. "I can speak for myself, Joan. Anyway, Mr. Lockner is fully aware of my opinions on the subject. I made it plain last night I consider it a wanton destruction of the past to deliberately choose a stretch of beach with one of the few remaining lighthouses in this area for his commercial venture."

"Very plain indeed," Drew agreed, barely concealing a smile.

Laurel rose abruptly. "Then why are you bothering me? Isn't it enough that you've won? Do you have to gloat?"

Joan's face paled as Drew rose leisurely. "I've come to remind you of the dinner party tonight. The one I mentioned to you in your apartment last night."

A gasp escaped Joan, but Laurel ignored it, saying icily, "I haven't forgotten."

"Would you like me to pick you up?" he persisted.

"That won't be necessary." The phone rang, and Laurel pointedly added, "Excuse me, but I'll have to get back to work now."

As soon as the door closed behind Drew's retreating back, Joan began making frantic signals to Laurel. When she finished her conversation on the phone, Joan was waiting. "You didn't tell me you invited him to your apartment last night," she exclaimed.

Laurel sighed. "Don't start that rumor, Joan. It was

his idea to drop by, and it will *never* happen again."
Glancing at the ancient wall clock she prompted, "Your
boss is going to be looking all over for you if you don't
hurry back."

"It's okay; I have an extra half hour coming. Tell me
why Mr. Lockner came by," she persisted.

Laurel sighed again. "It's something I don't want to
discuss."

Joan's eyes softened. "Can't you make him understand how you feel about the lighthouse?"

"He cares only about what he wants," she flared.

"If you ask me, I think he likes you. Didn't you notice
the way he kept looking at you?" Joan rushed the words
out, excitement glinting in her eyes.

Laurel shook her head disparagingly. "You see romance in everything!"

Joan glared obstinately. "Why are you invited to that
dinner? You're not on the town council or anything like
that."

"Maybe he wants a write-up in the paper about the
menu," Laurel said jokingly.

Joan smiled in return. "You may be right. Will you
be taking Howard with you?"

"Howard!" Laurel exclaimed. "No. It'll be strictly
business—no spouses or dates. But that reminds me. I
promised to call and tell Howard when to come by with
his new car."

"I hope you'll wear something pretty to Mr. Lockner's
house tonight," Joan replied, relentlessly returning to her
favorite subject. "I still think he's interested in you."

"Oh, will you stop it!" Laurel protested in mock ex-
asperation. "I thought you were my friend."

"I am. That's why I'm telling you—"

"Out, out! Back to work with you, or I'll tell Mayor Boggs that he'd better give you more work to do so you won't have so much time to read romances," Laurel threatened. "I think they're going to your head."

"Okay, I get the message. I'm leaving," Joan replied, adopting her best good-intentions-ignored look.

After Joan left, Laurel finished up a few last-minute tasks before phoning Howard. He arrived within an hour and escorted her out to his sparkling tan car, proudly pointing out various luxury features.

Laurel made an attempt to admire it enthusiastically and then settled back on the smooth upholstery when Howard suggested they take a ride. "Shall we drive out past the lighthouse?" he asked.

"No, not there." Laurel cringed inside, not wanting any reminders of Drew.

Howard misunderstood, awkwardly patting her knee. "It's rotten for you to lose it," he said.

"I'll survive." Laurel wished he would drop the subject.

Howard maneuvered the car out onto the road, heading away from the coast as he talked about a young patient who had kept him and his staff running during their busy morning.

"Do you remember that girl I was sitting next to at the club the other night?" he asked finally.

"The blonde?"

"Yes." Howard's fair skin turned faintly pink. "Her name is April Leeds, and she's a friend of Lockner's."

Laurel nodded. "I know. He sat next to me at the club while you two were talking."

"You said you didn't know him." Howard turned in surprise.

"I didn't; at least I didn't learn his identity until last night."

"April thinks the world of him." Howard's tone was slightly dejected.

"Money is very impressive," Laurel said sarcastically. "Is she planning on marrying him?"

"No!" Howard swerved to pass a small truck that was creeping along the road. "From what April says, he's not interested in marriage. Evidently his company was pretty broke at one time, and his fiancée dumped him to marry someone with more money."

"Tough luck." Laurel's curiosity was piqued, but she didn't particularly want to sympathize with Drew.

As usual Howard missed her sarcasm. "And that's not all," he continued. "His mother didn't give him too good an opinion about women either."

"Did she drop him on his head when he was a baby?"

"Laurel!" Howard's voice conveyed shock and outrage at her uncharacteristic hostility. "April has known Drew Lockner all her life. She said his mother was ruthless, always demanding more and more."

"Like mother, like son." Laurel tried to shut off memories of Drew's shadowed eyes when he had mentioned his father, "I suppose now she's urging him to gobble up all available beach property."

"She's dead. And he seems to be a confessed bachelor."

Laurel avoided Howard's glance, seizing on a sudden change of subject. "You must have done a lot of talking to April. Are you going to the club a lot these days?"

Howard flushed a dark red, stammering, "I'd rather spend time with you, Laurel, but you're always so busy..."

"I know," said Laurel quietly. "I haven't been much of a friend lately."

"I had hoped we'd be more than friends." Howard's voice held a note of finality.

"I'm flattered, but it's no use, Howard." Laurel's voice was warm with affection and concern. "I wish I were in love with you. You're such a nice person; you deserve someone who loves you."

Howard looked faintly relieved as he said, "So do you, Laurel."

CHAPTER ELEVEN

IT WAS ALMOST dusk by the time Laurel put the finishing touches on her appearance that evening. A reluctant curiosity lent speed to her fingers as she slipped the jacket of the turquoise silk dress over her shoulders, fastening the single button beneath the lace collar. She felt a desperate urge to be on her way, to confront Drew in his own environment, as though by seeing him totally in his role as head of the Lockner Development Corporation she could free herself from the potent spell that held her captive.

There had been no question of her not going to the dinner. As Drew had correctly surmised, she would do anything to save the lighthouse. Besides, Joan had called and told her the mayor expected her to attend. If she didn't show up, there would inevitably be questions, questions she did not want to be forced to answer.

She turned away from the mirror at last, satisfied that at least her appearance did nothing to give away the

157

turmoil raging inside her. The silk dress was immensely flattering, the soft skirt swirling around her slim legs, and the silver sandals lent her height and dignity.

The drive to Drew's address passed in a twilight haze. The directions Joan had given her led directly to the turn-off to a cluster of buildings along a beautiful stretch of beach. When she saw the sign reading "Shore Acres," Laurel remembered with shock that she had driven right past this place on Monday.

A wide drive curved inside the cluster of buildings, which were set in a semi-circle, their octagonal shapes giving each condominium unit a sweeping view of the water. The surrounding landscape looked surprisingly undisturbed, and the structures harmonized smoothly with the ocean front setting. There was none of the blatant commercial destruction she'd expected to see. Instead, as she parked the car and stepped out into the cool evening, she was immediately struck by the serenity of the grounds, the sense of luxury and privacy that character-ized the structures, and the meticulous planning that must have gone into creating the peaceful effect.

The building in the center was slightly taller than the others, Laurel noticed. That must be where Drew lived. With a sense of purpose she entered the quietly elegant lobby of the building and found the elevators.

A sudden thought struck her as she stood before the closed doors, waiting patiently for the elevator to arrive. It was not too late for her to turn back, to leave, to escape this meeting with Drew. But even as she thought it, she realized she could not do it. Only by seeing him here could she escape from her memories of his compelling domination.

The elevator rose to the penthouse with a swift, silent

passage of space that bespoke considerable expense in its construction. She emerged to find herself in a plush hallway, richly paneled in a dark, satiny wood. Taking a deep breath, she knocked lightly on the door in front of her.

It was opened at once, a composed, elderly woman greeting her with a smile and introducing herself as Mr. Lockner's housekeeper.

The mayor and the council members were already seated in the spacious living room. Laurel looked around slowly, her senses dazzled by the spectacularly beautiful room before her. An air of elegant simplicity character- ized its every feature, the total impression being one of breathtaking comfort and understated luxury.

Floor-to-ceiling windows comprised two entire walls, their gleaming surfaces unmarred by draperies of any kind. The midnight blue sky outside seemed almost a part of the room, the stars suspended from the ceiling itself.

The rest of the room was furnished in the cool, chang- ing colors of the sea; unobtrusive pieces were strategi- cally interspersed with empty spaces to enhance the airy atmosphere.

Drew came forward to shake her hand as she entered the room, his face impassive, his smile politely welcom- ing. Except for the housekeeper and one elderly council member, Laurel was the only woman present, her soft silky dress glowing like some wild exotic flower among the dark business suits around her.

Somehow she found herself seated, a glass containing an iced, faintly bitter drink in her hand. She was con- scious only of Drew, his lean, masculine body drawing her attention again and again even as she responded with a semblance of calm to the remarks directed her way.

He was wearing a navy blue suit tonight, as impeccably tailored as the one he'd worn the night before. His shirt was a pale blue, which contrasted sharply with his tanned neck and jaw. He was every inch the cool businessman; the casual, carefree stranger of the weekend was seemingly gone forever.

She tensed slightly as he walked over and sat down on the couch beside her, his shoulder brushing lightly against the sheer fabric of her dress. "Is this what you expected?" he asked, a curious smile lighting the depths of his eyes as he gestured sweepingly around the room.

"It's very beautiful," she admitted reluctantly. "Who decorated it for you?"

"You don't believe I could have done it myself?" This time his eyes held a hint of that familiar mocking gleam.

Laurel shrugged her shoulders lightly. "I really wouldn't know. After all, I know almost nothing about you."

He leaned more closely against her, his shoulder pressing her back into the soft depths of the sofa as he stared intently into her widened eyes. "On the contrary," he said smoothly. "I think you know me quite intimately."

Laurel's face flushed hotly, her skin suddenly prickling with a sensation that was not altogether unpleasant. She looked around hastily, praying no one else had heard his remark. To her relief, the housekeeper chose that moment to announce dinner.

Drew led the way into a dining room that was as beautiful as the living room they left behind. Gleaming crystal and silver were reflected in the ivory surfaces of the smooth china. The scent of fresh flowers filled the air, their brilliant petals making bright splashes of color around the room. She was seated immediately to Drew's right, her hopes of escaping his nearness during dinner completely dashed.

While the housekeeper brought around the first course, an exquisitely chilled array of tiny shrimp with a piquant sauce, Laurel was momentarily alone with her thoughts. Never had she imagined a scene of such opulent splendor as the one before her tonight.

Drew was obviously immensely successful; tonight she didn't find that hard to believe. He was far removed from the nonchalant, impractical artist in this setting. How had he changed so completely? Was it possible that he managed to combine these two facets of his personality, to "have it all," as he had told her it was possible to do?

Drew did not speak to her directly until they had almost finished the main course, a filet of striped bass wrapped in flaky puff pastry and served with braised artichokes.

Mayor Boggs was obviously enjoying the dinner to the utmost, his gleaming bald head bobbing up and down as he spoke loudly and gestured expansively. Pushing aside the major portion of her own rich meal, Laurel couldn't help wondering if Drew dined like this often. His powerfully fit muscles and lean form certainly didn't hint of it.

"Enjoying the food?" Drew's voice was low, loud enough to reach only her ears.

"It's delicious," she said politely.

"You seemed to enjoy our meals last weekend a good deal more," was his dry reply. She wondered what he was thinking, if he was remembering those shared meals with condescending amusement, comparing their rustic simplicity to this setting.

The dessert course seemed to pass in a sort of fog, Laurel lifting her fork automatically to her mouth, finding it difficult to keep her mind on the light anecdotes being tossed out around her. When would they get to the subject of the land, she wondered tiredly.

As they prepared to go back to the living room for coffee and liqueurs, Laurel felt a sudden need to escape for a few minutes. She sought out the housekeeper and followed her down a dimly lit corridor to a door at the far end. The woman swung it open with a smile, indicating there was a bathroom behind the door on the far side of the room. With another smile she turned and left.

Laurel entered the room slowly. It was dark except for a low lamp glowing on a table against one wall. Another window, like the ones in the living room, comprised one wall of the room. This one had dark blue drapes, the identical shade of the thick carpet beneath her feet. The drapes had been pulled back, leaving the view of the sky and sea outside unobstructed. Behind her the furnishings of the room displayed the same elegant simplicity that characterized the whole penthouse. A rich blue spread, also a blend of the colors of the ocean, adorned the large bed, and a low dresser stood against one wall.

Walking quietly, as if someone might hear, Laurel crossed to the dresser, her eyes drawn to the penciled sketches hanging above its smooth surface. With a small gasp of surprise she saw the signature in the bottom right corner. Drew had done these!

The sketches were stark and dramatic, scenes of the coast, which she recognized as that of the immediate area. So he hadn't lied about that! He might not make his living by drawing, but he was certainly an artist. Of course, now she remembered that Joan had said he'd studied art and architecture in college.

She turned away from the sketches reluctantly, crossing to stand beside the window, staring blankly at the twinkling stars in the dark sky outside.

Her confused mind fought against the niggling doubts that were beginning to form in the back of her mind. Maybe he hadn't been lying about everything. So far, the things he had told her had proved true. The problem was that there was a great deal he had omitted telling her, a few things he had deliberately kept from her.

Why hadn't he been honest about his identity? The only explanation she could come up with was the one she didn't want to believe. He hadn't told her because he had wanted to use her, to break down her highly vocal opposition to him by seducing her.

The door opened with a hushed murmur behind her and she turned swiftly. Drew shut the door behind him, leaning against it, blocking her exit with casual grace. They stared at each other without speaking for a long time, Laurel's mind a blank slate that refused to supply her with a single light remark.

"Do you like the view?" he asked finally. With swift deliberation he crossed the room and stood beside her.

"It's beautiful," she said, her voice echoing the effect he was having on her senses.

Laurel was conscious of his nearness in every cell of her body, the warm darkness wrapping around them like a web, enclosing them in a world of their own. "Your drawings are excellent," she murmured, searching for something to say.

"I didn't lie about that," he pointed out, his eyes watching her face intently.

"No," she agreed, turning back toward the window, watching the blinking lights of a lone sailboat that was gliding slowly along the distant horizon beyond the window. There was no way to deny the sudden rise of pleasure, the yearning of her senses, the irrefutable quickening of her pulse caused by his proximity.

"Does all this bother you, Laurel?" His voice was right beside her ear, his arm touching hers lightly.

"What do you mean?" She moved away slightly, her muscles tensing as he followed her. Her breathing had altered, its pattern erratic.

"The penthouse, the trappings of wealth. You've been looking at everything this evening as if you find it distasteful."

"There's nothing wrong with it," Laurel denied hastily. "After all, you're quite a successful man. Why not have the best?"

"Then why look at me as if you hate me? Why do your eyes flash every time they glance my way?" He ran one finger lightly along the curve of her arm, his touch barely penetrating the sheer fabric of her soft silk jacket. "Why do you draw away from me every time I touch you?"

"You're imagining things," she told him abruptly, pulling her arm away at the same time, making her words a lie.

"Don't you like my home?" Drew's voice was insistent, making it clear that he was not going to be satisfied with less than the truth.

"It's lovely." Laurel turned and looked at him, meeting his eyes directly for the first time all evening. "In fact, I feel I owe you an apology of sorts about one thing." Her voice faltered, and she hesitated.

"Yes?" His one word compelled her to go on, his body motionless, as if waiting for her answer.

"I've been unfair in one of my judgments." She rushed the words. "For months now I've been condemning your buildings, and yet this is the first time I've actually seen one, been inside one." She paused, her gaze dropping under his steady regard. "This is very nice. It fits in with the beach perfectly without destroying any of the natural beauty."

He was very quiet, and in the momentary silence she could tell his breathing had changed, was in fact almost as uneven as her own.

"Thank you," he said softly. Still he stood with that air of expectation, motionless, silent. What was he waiting for? Did he want her to go on, to apologize profusely, to elaborate on her compliment to his building?

Uncertainty made her voice harsh. "Isn't that enough for you, Drew?" She raised her eyes and regarded him steadily. "Do you want me to tell you it's all right for you to take my lighthouse?" Her voice rose a little as she stumbled on. "You know I'll never do that. You could have picked any spot along this coast, and yet you had to pick that one; now nothing else will do for you."

"No," he answered firmly, immovably. "I haven't changed my mind about buying that lighthouse. If anything, I'm more determined than ever."

Laurel turned away angrily, her body rigid and trembling. What had she expected? Men like Drew were relentless in the pursuit of what they wanted. When he didn't say anything more she started to walk past him. With one swift motion he blocked her way, his hands gripping both her arms, his fingers biting into her soft flesh.

She raised her face to his, searching the taut, unyielding line of his jaw, the firm contour of the lips that once had moved over hers with such feeling, such concern, such emotion. How was it possible for him to be so cold, so remote? Had it all been an act staged for her benefit?

"Don't fight me, Laurel." His voice was hushed and husky with feeling, his clasp on her arms tightening urgently as he pulled her against his chest, wrapped his arms around her, buried his face in her hair. Her skin tingled as his breath fanned her cheek, her ears were filled with the familiar sound of his whispered desire, her lips parted as his mouth found and laid claim to hers.

Holding her possessively against his solid, protective male length, he explored her mouth fully, uttering a low murmur of satisfaction against her lips when she yielded to his tender assault. Even as her mind rejected him, Laurel knew there was no resisting him, no holding back, the moment she felt his arms around her, the moment their lips met and clung.

Forgetful of the other guests waiting for them in the living room, forgetful of everything except this moment, she reached up and tangled her fingers in his thick hair, arching her body against his, seeking his caresses.

"For us the dream hasn't ended, Laurel." He whispered the words against her ear, his lips feathering along the tendrils of hair at her temple. His fingers found the fastening on her sheer jacket and slid it from her shoulders, his mouth trailing along the curve of her neck, probing the sensitive hollow at the base of her throat.

His hands moved over the delicate layer of fabric covering her hips, molding her body against his. "Have I told you how beautiful you're looking tonight?" Drew moved his head back just far enough to see her loosened hair, the silky dress, her bared shoulders. Laurel quivered as his hand slid the slender straps off her shoulders, his thumbs gently massaging the creamy rise of flesh above the disheveled bodice.

"Drew," she whispered, lost to the nameless desires raging inside her, aching with physical longing that made rational thinking impossible.

This time his kiss was fierce, carrying her with him on a tide of rising desire, setting off a chain of small explosions that had her arching against him, pressing light kisses along his firm jawline, tangling her fingers in his hair as he fondled her sensitized flesh.

A jarring knock on the bedroom door broke the spell. Drew caught his breath sharply, his hands tightening on her arms so she couldn't move away.

The door opened before they drew apart, and the housekeeper stood in the thin path of light filtering in from the hallway. Her features were impassive, not revealing by so much as the flicker of an eyelash that she was surprised by what she saw. "Telephone for you, sir. Will you take the call in your study?"

"I'll be there in a moment." Drew's voice was just as calm, quiet, and unembarrassed.

"Very well." The courteous older woman withdrew as swiftly as she had entered, pulling the door firmly shut behind her.

Drew's lips moved softly against hers again. "I've half a mind to ignore that and stay right here."

A small flutter of resistance rose in Laurel and she pushed him away, leaning back to look up at him. "You can't do that."

His eyes were faintly regretful, his touch light as he set her firmly away from him. "You're right, of course." His hands left her reluctantly, reaching to straighten his tie and smooth the work of her hands in his ruffled hair. "Will you still be here when I come back?" His eyes held hers, demanding her answer.

"What about your guests?" Laurel fought against the surge of happiness she felt as he spoke.

"I want to talk to you after they're gone," he replied, his face serious, his gaze tender. "Promise me you won't run away."

She smiled back, opening her mouth to answer him and then gasping softly when he dropped a swift, hard kiss on her parted lips. A moment later he had left the room.

Laurel walked back to the window. Somehow, things had to straighten themselves out. She couldn't go on the way she was, resisting Drew mentally but unable to deny him anything he asked of her. She had to break with him, refuse to ever see him again. But not tonight. She needed his touch, his embrace, his tenderness as he slowly aroused her. For tonight, she would cease fighting.

Opening the door to the bathroom, she went inside, her eyes widening with pleasure at the spacious counters and gleaming fixtures. Her hair was tumbled around her face, the silky fabric of her dress slightly disarrayed, her lipstick gone. With a few deft motions she managed to restore order to her appearance. If she didn't rejoin the guests soon, her disappearance would be too obvious to miss comment.

Taking a last lingering look out the wide window, she walked over and picked up her jacket, slipping it over her shoulders and fastening the small button below the collar. Her fingers froze as her eyes swept over the small table beside Drew's bed. In the dim light she couldn't be sure of what she was seeing.

Crossing the room swiftly, she picked up the black-and-white photograph resting on the polished surface. Her own face looked back at her, a photo she had never seen before. It had obviously been taken in front of the newspaper office. She was bending over her car, her face turned slightly away from the camera.

With shaking fingers Laurel turned the picture over and scanned the words on the back. "Martin Detective Agency," she read aloud slowly, her mind barely registering the date below the small stamp. Two weeks ago. Before Drew had ever come to the lighthouse.

Before she could stop herself she had shredded the photograph into little pieces, discarding them angrily on the wide bed.

It was all perfectly clear now. He'd known who she was all right, probably had known more about her than she knew about herself. She felt sick with rage as she thought of a detective agency watching her, prying into her life, photographing her! It had all been a deliberate attempt on his part to get the land.

She found it hard to believe he would go to such lengths. Not even Vince had been that despicable; he'd never engineered anything so elaborate to deceive her. At least she could find some small satisfaction in the fact that Drew had thought her opposition important enough

to worry about. Fury mingled with sick disappointment
in her confused mind, fury winning out in the end.

Grabbing her small evening bag, she clutched it firmly
and crossed the bedroom to the door. As she opened it,
the mayor was just emerging from a door on her left.
"Oh, there you are, Laurel," he said jovially. "I was
looking for you."

"I was in the bathroom," she said briefly, "I have a
slight headache."

His effusively sympathetic comments irritated her,
and she barely listened as he babbled, "Mr. Lockner has
some good news for us about the lighthouse. He's asking
us all to join him in the living room."

Seething with inner rage, Laurel nodded her head
politely, waiting until he had started off in the direction
of the living room before she hurried down the corridor
to the front door. Questions about her disappearance be
damned. She wasted no time before pressing the button
for the elevator, breathing a sigh of relief when it slid
to a smooth halt downstairs and she was able to escape
across the quiet lobby. Good news about the lighthouse,
she thought furiously. I'll just bet it's good news. If he
thought she would stay around and listen while he de-
clared his victory, he was in for a nasty shock.

CHAPTER TWELVE

AS SHE LEFT the cluster of condominiums far behind her, there was no doubt in Laurel's mind where she was headed. The lighthouse had always been her refuge, and she had never needed it more in her life than she did right now.

The moon was bright overhead, making the headlights of her car almost unnecessary as she drove through the velvet darkness of the night. With a sense of *déjà vu* she realized it was exactly one week ago tonight that she had driven out to the lighthouse to spend a quiet weekend.

Now that she knew the truth about Drew she felt almost calm. Her fiery rage had cooled, leaving behind it a sense of determination. Her temporary madness was over. The man she had begun to love did not exist—except in her own imagination. She had mistaken his every action, read her own meaning into every word he'd said.

James Andrew Lockner was now a reality in her mind.

And a man who would stoop to spying in order to get his way in a business deal had no part in her life. Her first instincts about him had turned out to be correct, and she forced herself to turn her back on the recent past, to forget the pleasure he had given her.

The lighthouse loomed on the horizon, its familiar bulk filling her with a sense of sadness. It was lost to her now; even if they left it standing it would never be the same. Once the old building was surrounded by condominiums, it would slowly crumble away. The present would overshadow the past, and she could no longer hold off the tide of events that would destroy the old landmark.

She parked her car outside the door, fumbling in her purse for the key and unlocking the massive door. It took a long time for her to light the lamp. First she had to search in the dark kitchen for matches, and then she found the fuel needed to be replenished. At last she had it glowing, its faint light barely penetrating the shadows surrounding her.

A sudden desire to see the sea from the top of the old structure assailed her, and kicking off her sandals, she grasped them in one hand and began climbing the staircase. The darkness slowed her progress, as did the fact she was carrying both her shoes and the lamp.

Reaching the top at last, she set the lamp on the floor off to one side, stopping to slip on her sandals as she remembered the broken glass that still lay on the floor. Staring out the window, she could see a faint glimmer of lights along the coast, here and there the signal lights of a small boat dotting the coastline. The sea was relatively calm tonight, its surface broken only by a few gently swelling waves.

It seemed as though hours had passed, but in reality

it hadn't been that long since she'd left Drew's apartment. By now he certainly would have discovered she was gone. Would he care since he'd gotten what he wanted?

A loud crash below made her jump up suddenly, her heart beating faster. The sound of footsteps echoed from the ground floor, and Laurel forced herself to go to the head of the stairs. "Who's there?" she called, her voice bouncing off the walls around her and echoing eerily in the darkness.

"Drew." His voice traveled up to her, strong and clear, determined.

When she didn't answer he said, "I knew you'd be here. You always come here whenever you're tired or upset, don't you?"

"Why are you here?" She heard the shrill note in her voice that instantly betrayed the inner turmoil she was trying to hide.

She listened to him coming up the stairs, his steps firm and measured, relentless in their pursuit. "I told you I wanted to talk to you, but you ran again," he accused, his voice closer this time. "You can't run anymore. This time you'll have to stay and talk."

Laurel waited at the top of the stairs without answering, her heart thudding painfully. Holding the lamp out over the staircase, she saw him come into the circle of light. He had taken off the dark suit jacket, his pale blue shirt was open at the collar. She moved back, waiting unwillingly until he stood beside her.

"Why did you run away this time?" His voice was patient, sounding as if he had all the time in the world.

"I found a photograph," Laurel angrily informed him. "A picture of me."

"The one you tore up," he agreed.

"Why did you have it, Drew? Why did you hire some-one to watch me, to find out about me?" Her voice was steadier now, and anger rushed her words.

He leaned against the window, his body carefully relaxed, his voice deliberately calm. "About a month ago I began to get curious about the person who was behind all those nasty articles about my bid for the lighthouse. So"—he shrugged lightly—"I hired someone to look into the matter for me."

"And what did you find out?" she asked bitterly. "That the editor was an overworked, frustrated widow who could probably be seduced into stopping her fight against you?"

"I didn't seduce you." Drew's voice was insistent, demanding her acquiescence. "We both wanted what happened."

Laurel didn't reply, his accurate assessment bringing a bitter lump to her throat. "So I made it easy for you," she said at last. "You didn't even have to try very hard."

He was silent, waiting for her to go on. "To hire a detective!" Laurel's voice was stiff with protest. "It seems like such a despicable, underhanded thing to do."

His voice was calm and unhurried. "The detective merely found out for me why you had such a personal interest in the lighthouse. The picture was his own idea, part of the package."

"You knew who I was the instant you saw me," Laurel burst out angrily.

"Not at the club. But I knew immediately you were someone I wanted to know better. Once I found out your identity, I knew very well there was no way I'd get to know you better if you learned who I was. And *that* you did make easy for me—you didn't even ask my last name."

Laurel couldn't say anything; she could only wait, helplessly, for whatever he said next. She felt her heart pounding furiously, her pulses throbbing.

He didn't say anything. Instead, he crossed the room in one swift stride, his arms pinning her against the glass behind her, his lips clamping down on hers in a kiss that was fire and seduction and domination. She struggled against him, pushing him away, flailing at him with her fists.

His laugh was low and exultant in her ear. "Oh, no," he said firmly, pinning her arms between them with one swift gesture. "You're not going to try to knock me out again." He went on kissing her, not ceasing the pressure of his mouth until she had stopped struggling, until she was kissing him back, a deep, heated urgency melting her against him, desire flowing like molten lava through her veins.

At last he drew away, his dark eyes gleaming triumphantly, his features revealing that he felt himself to be master of the situation.

"What do you want from me, Drew?" she asked angrily. "Is it because today is Friday? Are you back for another little weekend fling?"

He threw back his head and laughed, his eyes gleefully amused. "I want you every day of the week," he said. "Not just the weekends."

"I'm not interested," she fairly shouted. "Can't you get that through you head?" Her voice lacked the confidence she wanted to show him. Right now she needed every ounce of determination to fight against the slow seduction of his nearness, his kisses. Instead, she felt weak and defenseless, succumbing to the enchantment he could weave around her with one touch, one look.

"How can you say that?" He tugged her against him. "I haven't explained anything yet."

She beat at him fiercely, her fists caught in his firm grasp, her body melting against his as he kissed her again, slowly and thoroughly, until she was leaning weakly against him.

"Ready to listen?" he asked teasingly, running his fingers along her spine, pressing her intimately into the curve of his body.

"No," she retorted furiously, trying to get away from him and succeeding only in finding herself pressed even closer against him.

His voice continued blandly as if he hadn't noticed the interruption. "From the moment I saw you in that club, I haven't been the same. Then, once I learned who you were and met you here, of course I was interested in learning more of your thoughts about the lighthouse. But that isn't what kept me here last weekend," he broke off as she pushed against him again.

"You stayed because of your car and the storm," she accused him. "You didn't have any choice."

"It was a storm all right," he told her laughingly, "but the storm was inside, not outside. Within the first two hours you had me under your spell. When I kissed you up here and you knocked me down, I felt like some of that lightning outside had hit me as well.

"I admit it may seem strange," Drew continued, smiling down at her. "I'd never met anyone so determined as you, so sure of herself, so fiery. And you wanted only what you thought was rightfully worth fighting for—for others as well as yourself. You were even willing to do it all yourself, take the risks yourself, not sit back and expect anyone else to fight your battles for you."

She was touched by the sincerity of his words and tone, and she momentarily forgot that *he* was the Goliath she had slung her pebbles at. Unable to speak, she started to shift out of his embrace, but he wrapped his arms more tightly around her and continued explaining.

"You were so serious about everything; I felt I had to stay around and wait for you to smile, to laugh about something with me." He kissed her lightly, his eyes alight with laughter. "We're going to have an exciting life," he told her confidently. "People as strong-willed as we never have it easy. We'll fight and we'll make up, but things will never be boring."

"We?" Laurel echoed shakily.

"Us," he agreed, kissing her again in a disturbingly distracting manner. She pushed away, trying to free herself from the close embrace in which he held her, trying to think.

"Don't you understand?" she argued weakly. "I don't even like you."

"Nonsense," he stated arrogantly. "You love me."

"That's ridiculous!" she flared sharply, her heart pounding.

"Oh, is it?" He smoothed back her hair, framing her face with one hand and forcing her to look up at him. "Face it," he murmured soothingly. "We go together like a bear and honey, like pigs and mud, like—"

"Bare skin and water?" she muttered, laughing helplessly, reluctantly.

"Exactly." He bent over as if to kiss her again, but Laurel pushed him away.

"We're opposites in every way," she argued. "You think only of the future; I value the past. You're wealthy; I never have enough left to meet expenses. Don't you understand? We come from different places, we're going different places."

"That's where you're wrong," he assured her stubbornly. "From now on we're together. I'm not letting you out of my arms again."

"That could get a little uncomfortable," Laurel murmured wryly.

He slid one hand along her shoulder, twisting away the thin jacket and caressing the smooth bare skin of her shoulder. "I don't think you'll have any complaints."

"You're going too fast," she protested helplessly. "What about my lighthouse?"

Drew pulled her down to sit with him on the floor, swinging her body across his lap until she was cradled against his shoulder. "You didn't stay to hear my news tonight."

"The mayor told me. You got the land." Laurel stiffened, her muscles tensed as she waited for his answer.

"I bought the land all right," his voice whispered against her hair. "Me. Not the Lockner Development Corporation. This is a personal investment."

Laurel stared up at him disbelievingly. "What about your condominiums?"

"We'll build them farther down the coast. My company has been looking at several pieces of land along here. There's a beautiful strip of beach just south of here. It took me all week, but I finally talked my board of directors into agreeing to buy one of the other properties."

"What will you do with the lighthouse?" Laurel avoided

his eyes as she asked the question.

He tightened his grip on her, leaning his cheek against her soft hair. "It's yours," he whispered.

"What?" Laurel sat up with a start, looking at him incredulously. Her eyes narrowed with suspicion. "There are strings attached, of course."

"Just one." Drew eyed her, a slightly calculating glint in his eyes. "Me. You'll have to marry me." His voice was dry, matter-of-fact.

"You're pretty damn sure of yourself!" she flared, the blood singing in her veins.

"I'm sure I love you," he agreed, his eyes suddenly serious, his face intent. "From the first moment we met, I've been caught under your spell."

"Love," Laurel retorted harshly. "Isn't that another name for domination?"

"You have a lot to learn about love, Laurel." Drew pulled her closer against him, kissing her lightly. "And I want to be the one who teaches you how magical it can be."

"We don't even know each other." Laurel felt herself being pulled deeper and deeper. "Nobody falls in love that fast."

"I know all the important things about you," he retorted significantly. His voice was laughing, amused, as he supplied, "I know you don't snore, you don't use all the hot water, and you squeeze the toothpaste from the bottom, exactly like I do."

"You really are obstinate!" She turned to look at him, her eyes wide.

"I also know," he ignored her as he continued, "that you have a very nasty temper."

"No worse than yours!" she flared.

"See what I mean?" he grinned broadly. He stroked the length of her slim legs, his hands soothing the taut muscles, his lips teasing gently at the corner of her mouth. Laurel turned her mouth to his kiss, putting her arms around his neck, not making any attempt to escape as he continued his seductive assault on her senses.

When his mouth left hers, she protested softly. Drew lifted her chin with one finger, his touch insisting she look up at him. "Why did you leave me out on the beach?" he asked her, his eyes darkly intent, allowing her no chance to evade the question. "When I woke up you were gone. No good-bye, no explanation."

This time she knew she couldn't escape. She would have to admit the truth honestly, let him see how vulnerable she was to him. "I was afraid," she whispered faintly.

"Afraid?" His eyes were questioning, holding hers with an intent gaze. "Afraid I'd be like Vince?"

"I suppose your detective told you about him." Laurel pulled away slightly, her muscles tensing again.

"Enough to provide me with a good explanation for why you ran every time I got close to you," he said. "I know what it's like to feel betrayed by someone you thought you loved. But it will never be that way with us." His fingers played lightly along her spine, curving around her slender waist. "I love you, Laurel. You're a dream come true." His voice was husky with feeling. "Everything about you seems made to order, a perfect match. I can't believe my good fortune. Making love to you was the icing on the cake, but what we have between us goes much farther than that." Drew's voice stopped, his mouth claiming hers in a long, possessive kiss, leaving her breathless and shaken.

Laurel knew the moment had come for her to trust her own feelings. "No wonder you were so patient," she whispered. "I was so afraid of loving you, and you were so patient." Her voice was hesitant and uncertain at first, growing stronger as she felt his instant response. "But I did love you—I do love you."

This time their kiss had the fire of mutual trust, of love recognized and acknowledged. The flames of passion leaped high between them, their mouths meeting in deep union, their hands seeking to touch, to caress, to give and receive.

She rested in his arms, looking up at him in the faint light, tracing a pattern with her fingertips along the muscled planes of his chest. A sudden thought made her sit up and say firmly, "I'll never give up my paper!"

"I'll never ask you to," Drew said just as firmly. "It's part of you. I know that, and I love that." He traced one finger along her cheek. "But you'll have to hire an assistant. From now on your evenings and weekends are going to be very busy."

"I'd never allow you to interfere, you know," Laurel warned.

"I wouldn't dream of it." Drew pulled her back against him, stroking her lightly. "The paper is all yours, and it will always be that way. It's part of your background, and I hope you can make it a part of the lives of all the children we have."

"You're going too fast again," she said laughingly. "One thing at a time." His answer was to kiss her again, lightly at first, then with deepening passion.

"When will you marry me?" he asked her finally. "I

don't want to wait too long. You might change your mind."

"There's no chance of that," she promised lightly, her eyes serious.

"We'll get married as soon as we can, and then take a long honeymoon," he stated.

"Where shall we go?"

"How about here?" he whispered against her lips. "This is the perfect place, if you don't mind the lack of electricity and a few other inconveniences."

"Hmm," she murmured, kissing him along the side of his jaw, running her fingers around the open collar of his shirt, melting against him.

"When?" he asked huskily.

"We've got the whole weekend!" She laughed softly as his lips closed over hers, their touch a seal and a promise.

WATCH FOR
6 NEW TITLES EVERY MONTH!

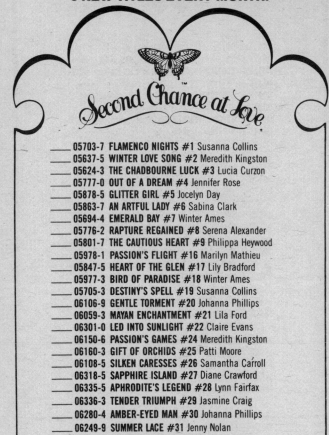

Second Chance at Love

____ 06401-7 PRIMITIVE SPLENDOR #41 Katherine Swinford
____ 06424-6 GARDEN OF SILVERY DELIGHTS #42 Sharon Francis
____ 06521-8 STRANGE POSSESSION #43 Johanna Phillips
____ 06326-6 CRESCENDO #44 Melinda Harris
____ 05818-1 INTRIGUING LADY #45 Daphne Woodward
____ 06547-1 RUNAWAY LOVE #46 Jasmine Craig
____ 06423-8 BITTERSWEET REVENGE #47 Kelly Adams
____ 06541-2 STARBURST #48 Tess Ewing
____ 06540-4 FROM THE TORRID PAST #49 Ann Cristy
____ 06544-7 RECKLESS LONGING #50 Daisy Logan
____ 05851-3 LOVE'S MASQUERADE #51 Lillian Marsh
____ 06148-4 THE STEELE HEART #52 Jocelyn Day
____ 06422-X UNTAMED DESIRE #53 Beth Brookes
____ 06651-6 VENUS RISING #54 Michelle Roland
____ 06595-1 SWEET VICTORY #55 Jena Hunt
____ 06575-7 TOO NEAR THE SUN #56 Aimee Duvall
____ 05625-1 MOURNING BRIDE #57 Lucia Curzon
____ 06411-4 THE GOLDEN TOUCH #58 Robin James
____ 06596-X EMBRACED BY DESTINY #59 Simone Hadary
____ 06660-5 TORN ASUNDER #60 Ann Cristy
____ 06573-0 MIRAGE #61 Margie Michaels
____ 06650-8 ON WINGS OF MAGIC #62 Susanna Collins
____ 05816-5 DOUBLE DECEPTION #63 Amanda Troy
____ 06675-3 APOLLO'S DREAM #64 Claire Evans
____ 06680-X THE ROGUE'S LADY #69 Anne Devon
____ 06687-7 FORSAKING ALL OTHERS #76 LaVyrle Spencer
____ 06689-3 SWEETER THAN WINE #78 Jena Hunt
____ 06690-7 SAVAGE EDEN #79 Diane Crawford
____ 06691-5 STORMY REUNION #80 Jasmine Craig

All of the above titles are $1.75 per copy

Available at your local bookstore or return this form to:

SECOND CHANCE AT LOVE
Book Mailing Service, P.O. Box 690, Rockville Cntr., NY 11570

Please send me the titles checked above. I enclose _____ .
Include 75¢ for postage and handling if one book is ordered; 50¢ per book for
two to five. If six or more are ordered, postage is free. California, Illinois, New
York and Tennessee residents please add sales tax.

NAME _____

ADDRESS _____

CITY_____ STATE/ZIP_____
Allow six weeks for delivery.   SK-41

____ 06692-3 **THE WAYWARD WIDOW** #81 Anne Mayfield
____ 06693-1 **TARNISHED RAINBOW** #82 Jocelyn Day
____ 06694-X **STARLIT SEDUCTION** #83 Anne Reed
____ 06695-8 **LOVER IN BLUE** #84 Aimée Duvall
____ 06696-6 **THE FAMILIAR TOUCH** #85 Lynn Lawrence
____ 06697-4 **TWILIGHT EMBRACE** #86 Jennifer Rose
____ 06698-2 **QUEEN OF HEARTS** #87 Lucia Curzon
____ 06850-0 **PASSION'S SONG** #88 Johanna Phillips
____ 06851-9 **A MAN'S PERSUASION** #89 Katherine Granger
____ 06852-7 **FORBIDDEN RAPTURE** #90 Kate Nevins
____ 06853-5 **THIS WILD HEART** #91 Margarett McKean
____ 06854-3 **SPLENDID SAVAGE** #92 Zandra Colt
____ 06855-1 **THE EARL'S FANCY** #93 Charlotte Hines
____ 06858-6 **BREATHLESS DAWN** #94 Susanna Collins
____ 06859-4 **SWEET SURRENDER** #95 Diana Mars
____ 06860-8 **GUARDED MOMENTS** #96 Lynn Fairfax
____ 06861-6 **ECSTASY RECLAIMED** #97 Brandy LaRue
____ 06862-4 **THE WIND'S EMBRACE** #98 Melinda Harris
____ 06863-2 **THE FORGOTTEN BRIDE** #99 Lillian Marsh
____ 06864-0 **A PROMISE TO CHERISH** #100 LaVyrle Spencer
____ 06865-9 **GENTLE AWAKENING** #101 Marianne Cole
____ 06866-7 **BELOVED STRANGER** #102 Michelle Roland
____ 06867-5 **ENTHRALLED** #103 Ann Cristy
____ 06868-3 **TRIAL BY FIRE** #104 Faye Morgan
____ 06869-1 **DEFIANT MISTRESS** #105 Anne Devon
____ 06870-5 **RELENTLESS DESIRE** #106 Sandra Brown
____ 06871-3 **SCENES FROM THE HEART** #107 Marie Charles
____ 06872-1 **SPRING FEVER** #108 Simone Hadary
____ 06873-X **IN THE ARMS OF A STRANGER** #109 Deborah Joyce
____ 06874-8 **TAKEN BY STORM** #110 Kay Robbins
____ 06899-3 **THE ARDENT PROTECTOR** #111 Amanda Kent

All of the above titles are $1.75 per copy

Available at your local bookstore or return this form to:

SECOND CHANCE AT LOVE
Book Mailing Service, P.O. Box 690, Rockville Cntr., NY 11570

Please send me the titles checked above. I enclose _____
Include 75¢ for postage and handling if one book is ordered; 50¢ per book for
two to five. If six or more are ordered, postage is free. California, Illinois, New
York and Tennessee residents please add sales tax.

NAME _____

ADDRESS _____

CITY_____ STATE/ZIP_____
Allow six weeks for delivery.   **SK-41**

WHAT READERS SAY ABOUT
SECOND CHANCE AT LOVE BOOKS

"Your books are the greatest!"
  —*M. N., Carteret, New Jersey**

"I have been reading romance novels for quite some time, but the SECOND CHANCE AT LOVE books are the most enjoyable."
  —*P. R., Vicksburg, Mississippi**

"I enjoy SECOND CHANCE [AT LOVE] more than any books that I have read and I do read a lot."
  —*J. R., Gretna, Louisiana**

"I really think your books are exceptional...I read Harlequin and Silhouette and although I still like them, I'll buy your books over theirs. SECOND CHANCE [AT LOVE] is more interesting and holds your attention and imagination with a better story line..."
  —*J. W., Flagstaff, Arizona**

"I've read many romances, but yours take the 'cake'!"
  —*D. H., Bloomsburg, Pennsylvania**

"Have waited ten years for *good* romance books. Now I have them."
  —*M. P., Jacksonville, Florida**

*Names and addresses available upon request